SLEEP TIGHT

SLEEP TIGHT

Horrors of my Dreamland

MORGAN SALLEE

Morgan Allynn Sallee

Breathe

I rushed to my locker and struggled to get the lock open.

"Come on open," I muttered to myself as I failed at the combination once again. I managed to finally get it right and I tugged my locker open and grabbed my bag. I rushed to my classroom and threw myself down with a breathless sigh. We received an announcement that we weren't allowed to leave the building. There was an atmosphere of confusion. There was a murmur that washed through the room.

"As you're all aware there was a storm predicted today," Mrs. Brook said. "Well, we've been keeping a close eye on the weather reports and all of the faculty believe it would be safer for you guys to stay here until the storm passes over. Nearby cities and towns have reported severe flooding and some multi-story houses have been completely flooded out," She added smiling. "You're all free to roam the school," She finished sitting down at her desk.

She had short blonde hair that came to just under her jaw. She was around 40 years old and had a round face with visible frown lines. She was a rather kind person which left people wondering why she always looked so angry. She had light brown eyes and wore thick, brown, rectangular glasses.

I left the room and saw everyone else talking with each other laughing and talking about how awesome it was to spend the night in the school. I looked around and spotted my friends Sam, Drew, and Sean. I ran over holding my bag with one hand and holding down my boobs with my other. Talk about busty teen problems. When I slowed down I let my hands fall to my sides.

"Thoughts?" I asked, my hands buried in my pockets.

"I think it's pretty cool, I guess," Sam said. "I would rather be home on my computer, but I'm worried that our parents aren't coming to pick us up, we're literally stuck here," she added.

Sam had shoulder length curly bleach blonde hair. She was really pretty despite having acne. She did a lot of after school activities.

"I don't really have an opinion, I mean, we're stuck in school," Drew said simply, he seemed a bit checked out of the conversation.

Drew was tall and stickish. He was tan with brown hair and brown eyes. He had a crooked, goofy smile.

"I'm sure we'll find a way to have fun," I grinned, I reached out and touched Sam's elbow. We talked among ourselves for a little while. We pretty much sat in one of the locker bays and worked on our homework, concluding that we wouldn't have to do it when we got home. As we worked we could hear the gentle pitter shift to a roaring monsoon. We slowly grew anxious as the roar never waned.

"Are you guys worried at all?" I asked. I was hoping that talking about it would make it a bit less nerve racking.

"Not really, schools always are dramatic when it comes to stuff like this," I found myself getting up and moving towards the window of the school. The parking lot was flooded, cars had water almost to the bottom of their windows.

"Oh my god," I murmured. Sam, Drew, and our friend Shaun made their way to the window I was standing at.

"That's insane, I wonder if its getting in any of the doors?" Sean asked. He had short buzzed hair, he was short but had a body for football.

"I need everyone to go to the third floor immediately," A teacher demanded, panic apparent in her voice. I felt a pit form in my stomach; worry making my stomach heave. We obeyed the teacher, sharing glances of concern and confusion. I began to make my way to the stairwell, hearing my friends shuffling behind me.

When I turned around at the foot of the stairs I noticed Drew managed to slip away from the group.

"Where did Drew go?" I asked Sam and Shaun.

"He said he needed to get something out of his locker," Shaun responded, shrugging. The teacher pursed her lips, seemingly thinking what I was thinking.

"I'll get him," I said quickly, rushing to his locker bay. I paused when I noticed my pant legs getting wet.

I looked down and noticed that I was standing in about half an inch of water. I continued on my way with a newly discovered panic. I spotted him struggling with his lock.

"We need to get upstairs," I said firmly, marching up to him and grabbing his shirt.

"I need to get something out of my locker," He responded, resisting my grip and pushing me away.

"Is it really that important, the hallway is actively flooding," I hissed, pointing at the water that was now around our ankles and quickly rising. He ignored me and continued to fumble with his locker lock.

"Drew, we need to go!" I hissed swatting at his hands. I looked around and the floor was completely empty; a chill ran down my spine from how uneasy I felt. I grabbed his arms and gave a hard pull.

"Will you stop it! Just trust me that it's important," Drew barked. I was thrown off guard by his response to me. I let go and rubbed my hands on my thighs.

"Fine, if you want to stick around, be my guest," I said, turning on my heels and going to walk away.

"Fuck!" He shouted and I heard him punch his locker.

I looked over my shoulder at him, his head resting against the locker as he fumbled with the lock again. When I turned around I saw an almost wave surge through the hallway and the water grew murkier as the water quickly rose above my hips to my waist.

"We need to go!" I shouted over the rushing of water. I tried grabbing his shoulder and pulling him away from his locker. He gave the latch one last tug and sighed. Turning to follow me. The water rushed around our chests, soon it was going to be easier to just swim through the water than walk.

"Wait!" Drew shouted. I paused and looked behind me, he looked like he was struggling with something under the water.

"What's wrong?" I shouted, my stomach twisted with anxiety, I knew what words were coming next, but I wasn't ready to hear them.

"I'm stuck!" He cried out. I made my way back to him and dove under the water. He closed his jacket in the locker. I popped back up. The water was rising so fast, it was now around our necks.

"You closed your jacket in the door, what's the combo?" I asked, I was struggling to stay above water and speak. I felt my clothes weighing me down and I couldn't properly kick with my shoes on.

"N-Nine – Thirty-Six – Five," He stammered. I put my head under the water and fumbled with the lock. It wouldn't be released. I felt the click, but the lock wouldn't open; It was stuck. When I came back up Drew was looking up at the water rising quickly. Soon he would be fully submerged. I grabbed the zipper of his jacket and tried pulling it, hoping it would rip or come free, but nothing was budging.

I resurfaced.

"What the Fuck!" I shouted. I began to grow frantic and tried forcing the zipper down, it refused to move. When I resurfaced I hit my head on the ceiling. I took one last breath before diving down for the final time. He was trying to pull his arms into his sleeves. He was freaking out although he was trying to remain calm. I saw the look on his face. He was running out of air. His chest was twitching; he was about to breathe out. Drew struggled to pull himself out of the hoodie.

He exhaled and gasped for air. His eyes widened as he continued to try and gasp for air. He began to claw at his throat. I just watched him as he struggled for air. He flailed about, trying to escape to the surface. Then he just stopped, his body just hovered, motionless. I was pulled out of my trance when I noticed the burning in my own lungs. I swam for the stairs, looking for air pockets. I broke the surface at the staircase to the second floor.

"Help!" I screamed the second I got on solid ground, gasping for air.

"What happened, sweetheart?" A teacher asked, rushing cupping my face.

"D-D-D..." I couldn't make words, all I could do was sputter out nonsense as I stood there trembling like a scared animal. It should have been me.

The Game

I got out of the car; my city recently built a new sports arena that I found myself staring up at. It was supposed to be special because every sport could be played there. I'm not much of a sports person but I was invited for a group study for some reason. I had nothing better to do so I decided to go. There were other cars so I knew I wasn't the first person there. I made my way to the entrance; the doors were large and heavy. When I got inside, I was engulfed in cold air. I almost immediately was greeted by a woman.

She had long curly red hair with pretty, green eyes.

"Hi, I'm Cindy, you are?" She asked, looking down at a clipboard in her hands.

"Kat," I replied. I watched her eyes dance around before her smile grew ever so slightly.

"Ah, you're right here, follow me please," She said, pointing at the board then walking down a hallway. I followed her, looking around and taking in. The entire inside was white; the walls were made of white tiles and the floor was made of white linoleum with blue specks. There were giant windows overlooking the parking lot and the city.

"So, what do you think of the building?" She asked as we walked down the hallway. The hall had a small slant up and you circled around over and over.

"It's big," I responded, my voice echoing up the hall; it was quiet.

"Well, we house arenas for all competitive sports," She said.

"That's cool, but what does that have to do with me?" I questioned. The question was ignored and I was led into a small room. There were a handful of other people there.

The room was made of large, white, painted bricks, and the tile was the same white as in the hallway. The tables were heavy stone tables on wooden legs lined with 2 cheap metal chairs.

"Today you're all going to be experimenting with a new kind of competitive gaming," Cindy said smiling as she began to hand out thick packets. "This is just a formality, but I need you to sign these waivers saying you won't sue us for any physical or mental damage," She added with a forced chuckle. She handed out pens and we all signed it, everyone read the contracts at varying speeds. When we each handed her our forms she made sure that we all signed them.

"What exactly are we doing?" A dark-haired girl asked from the back corner.

"I'm glad you asked that, Maddy, you are testing a form of VR," Cindy started. "It tests your physical skills in these situations, you'll be wearing special suits and helmets that prevent any damage or pain," She continued. "The way this will work, we'll load you into a simulation of various game genres, etc. The thing is, you must never, ever take off your suits," She said firmly.

"What happens if we take the suit off?" A man asked, standing behind me. He was tall and lean with shaggy brown hair.

"You'll feel the full effects of what these games have to offer," She whispered. Her eyes looked dead despite having a large smile on her face. He nodded. "So, let's get you all into your suits and ready for the first simulation," She said, clapping her hands excitedly. We followed her out a different door than the one I entered. This hallway was different shades of blue that blended together in a beautiful hypnotizing mosaic of the ocean meeting the sky. The hallway went on for a long time and as we walked I looked out the window. The sky had grown overcast rather quickly, and we seemed a bit higher up than I remembered.

We entered another completely white room with changing rooms, also completely white. We were handed white and blue suits that admittedly looked tacky and weird. We all stripped down to our underwear and began tugging the suit on. The fabric felt strange, it was stretchy and easily pulled over our bodies, but once it was on, it felt suffocating.

"It's so hard to move," I muttered under my breath as I tried to stretch the fabric.

"That will go away once you're in the simulation, it will feel as if you're wearing nothing" Cindy smiled happily. Once we were all suited up, Cindy opened yet another door that led into a room that was the most pristine and perfect white. I couldn't tell where the walls ended, the floor started, and where the ceiling was. It just looked like a white void that could be endless. I was the first to step inside the room.

Upon stepping inside, I realized this was a giant sphere. The floor was rounded, and it was hard to keep my balance; almost sliding and falling. One by one, the others followed and they too, stumbled and struggled to catch their balance. Cindy shut the door behind us and the door seemed to vanish into the void. I heard her voice over the intercom.

"Don't mind the floor, it'll be flat in no time, what would you like to try out first?" She asked.

"Horror," I said looking up at the sky. I watched the white room shift into a dark concrete tunnel, there was water up to our knees. There were a couple flashlights on the table. I grabbed a flash light and shined it down the hallway.

"You don't have to worry about monsters, this focuses on jump scares and how people get affected by sounds," Cindy explained.

"Sounds good," I said, shining my light about. It was warm and muggy, the air was moist and heavy. We silently shared looks of fear and nervousness.

I started down the hallway; water sloshing echoed through the chamber. We were only able to see a few feet ahead of ourselves, the flashlight only had a faint beam. We soon approached a fork in the tunnel.

"What way?" I asked. We spent about five minutes debating which way we should go. We decided to split up. Four each way. I was worried that eventually, we would all be split up to the point of going through this maze alone, a race to find the end. The water grew deeper, rising to our waist as we walked through the winding dark halls. Eerie laughter sent shivers down my spine and there was a blur of flashlight beams shooting around trying to find who laughed. Water sloshed but it was impossible to tell where it was coming from.

"Cindy, how close are we to the end?" I shouted up at the ceiling hoping she would hear.

"You aren't far, but not close either. The other group has completely split up," She replied ominously.

"What kind of answer is that?" A man named Caleb asked. For a few brief seconds the silence was piercing. We continued forward the tunnel weaving to the left and right before coming to four tunnels. They were dimly lit with torches.

"I think they want us to separate," I murmured. I noticed there were other tunnels connecting to this room. I was wondering if there were different scares down those tunnels. I wondered if at any moment the others would emerge from the tunnel, while also wondering if they already were ahead of us.

"Do you think it's safe to split up?" A girl named Marilyn asked.

"That's what the suits are for," I responded, trying to sound confident.

I started down one of the tunnels. The light from the torch didn't go far and soon the only thing I could see was the yellowish-white circle on the damp floor. The darkness seemed to dim the light. I heard one of the girls screaming and the slapping of footsteps on wet cement getting louder as if the steps were coming towards me. I spun around seeing if I could see anyone. Pitch black. I turned back around and jumped back almost falling down; there was no longer the endless tunnel I was walking down. I turned back to where I came. There was another tunnel jutting out to the side, I had a straight shot through the other tunnels. I walked down the newly formed passageway, my heart was pounding so hard I could hear it over my footsteps. I began walking down the next tunnel, trying to find one of the others who were in this project.

I heard another scream and I spun around once more, looking for whoever was screaming. When I turned to head back down the tunnel it was yet another sudden dead end. I felt my stomach tighten.

"Cindy, what's going on?" I shouted. I felt my hands shaking and my blood pulsing through my body.

"There appears to be a glitch in the code, there is a monster in there with you, but I can't pinpoint the location, it is appearing all over the map, but you're the only one left," Cindy murmured. She sounded worried. "I suggest you run, your life may depend on it," She murmured. I started running down the tunnel hoping that I would find some of the others as I went on. Then I saw something move, it wasn't a person though. It was tall and pitch black, it would blend in with the darkness if my light wasn't shining on it. Its fingers were long, its nails were jagged. He held one of the girls, she was dead though, her eyes were glossy and vacant, she just dangled there like a doll.

I stood watching, frozen in fear as it lifted her even higher in the air as its jaw opened, unhinging, showing rows and rows of sharp, yellow and orange teeth. It lowered her into his mouth and bit off at the torso, its teeth cut through her like scissors with paper. As it chewed up her lower body, blood spurted and spewed from its mouth. Her organs dangled from her top half. I couldn't feel my knees as my legs violently shook, barely able to sustain my weight. I felt my heart in my throat.

"Run!" Cindy screamed, pulling me out of a trance of horror. I launched myself at the nearest door and slammed it shut behind me.

"What the fuck was that thing!" I shouted, I hunched over with my hands on my knees as my stomach churned and shifted. I didn't want to believe what I saw. I felt my eyes sting with tears; My brain cycled through every emotion, I was happy I lived, I couldn't believe that a monster killed her, I can't believe they didn't do more thorough testing, I should have ignored the invitation...

"We removed the code but somehow it found its way back and you have to leave now," She said. Within a minute the world began to fade away around me and I was back in the all white room. I tore the suit off of my body, not caring if I damaged it.

"I'm going the fuck home and I'm going to tell everyone about this!" I shouted pulling my clothes back on. Cindy shushed me and pulled me out of the room and into a different one.

"Somehow, it's no longer part of the simulation, this is real fucking life," She whispered. She grabbed my hand and pulled me into the hallway and we ran through the halls. Our footsteps echoed off the walls, I also heard the menacing footsteps of the monster. Cindy pulled me into a room and locked the door. She hid in a closet and I hid in a small cabinet. The footsteps grew louder as they neared. My heart was beating a mile a minute, I felt like I couldn't breathe.

I heard the door to our room slam open. I flinched and I heard Cindy whimper from across the room. The footsteps hastened before the floor shook from the wood breaking. I heard her gurgling and gagging, I was trying my hardest to stay quiet. When Cindy fell silent it would have been less unsettling if I heard something. The room was dead silent, the only thing I heard was the buzz of lights. It felt like hours waiting for any kind of indication it was gone. I thought maybe I was crazy; my body cramped and ached being in the same position for so long. I didn't want to risk breaking the silence for fear of it finding me. Then I heard it leave, slowly as if it was menacing me, daring me to move too soon. I waited for it to fall silent after its steps faded away.

When I got out, I only glanced at Cindy's body, not wanting to see what horrible fate she suffered. I walked out of the room silent, I was so aware of my own breathing, my steps and my clothes. I had to find the door. I had no idea where I was in this building. I had no idea where I could go, where I could hide. I walked around aimlessly, making sure my steps were as silent as possible. I rounded a sharp bend and stopped dead in my tracks, there it was. We gazed at each other, unsure when to make the next move; who would make the next move. I turned on my heels and sprinted down the hallway, I heard it bounding right behind me. The walls and floor seemed to shake with every step it took. Then I felt it. Its claws dug into my head. Its nails sunk deep into my skin. It squeezed harder.

Darkness

I left work late, having had to clean up. I decided to take a short cut through a wooded area that got me to a bus stop faster than walking around. As I walked down the path I felt unusually cold, what once was a crisp chill was now a paralyzing cold. The trees curled into different shapes and shadows. I felt uneasy given how late in the night it was. I heard the crunch of leaves under my feet but I kept my ears peeled for any noise that wasn't me. About 20 minutes into the walk I began to hear quiet voices off in the trees, they seemed so far yet just out of sight. I broke into a light jog, wondering whether or night I wanted to find out who or what those voices belonged to. I couldn't quite hear what the voices were saying. The voices never grew closer nor faded away, I was desperate to see the light from the road soon.

I found myself extremely on edge, the slightest sound sent my heart racing. I heard someone laugh which made my stomach somersault. It seemed so careless, it almost sounded childlike, but it made me feel even more uneasy. I was hoping it was some kind of sick joke some kids were playing on me. I hastened my pace, trying to get out as quickly as I could, then I could see it, light. I pushed my way through the bushes and branches, squinting to see if there were any people, as I got closer I was able to make out more and more people who were gathered around a fire. They were talking and laughing. I hoped these people were the people I heard and I got carried away with fear. When they turned to look at me I was immediately put back on guard.

They each had a sweet smile on their face. They all had the same unsettling smile, and they stopped their conversations to look at me. It didn't take too long for someone to approach me.

"Who are you?" She asked, her pitch high and artificial.

"I'm Carrie, who are you?" I asked hoping that they might be able to help me.

"That doesn't really matter," She smiled. I forced myself to smile back although I wanted to run the other way. There was something so unsettling by the silence and everyone staring at me. "Are you lost?" She asked to walk over to another girl who handed her a small bag. She dumped a good amount of powder in her hand. It was a deep black with a Purple tint. There were specks of what looked like glitter.

"I'll need you to relax for a moment," She murmured, she turned to face me, before I could turn to run away, she lifted her hand and blew the powder in my face. I flinched back. I cried out as the powder got in my eyes. I sputtered as it got in my mouth, it tasted awful and my eyes burned violently. I stumbled back as I viciously rubbed my eyes.

"What the fuck?" I muttered. I tried opening my eyes, everything was blurry; I felt tears streaming down my cheeks. I tried squinting, but the effort was in vain, it only caused more tears to run down my face. All I saw was darkness and a few blurry lights. I used my shirt to try wiping my eyes. Soon my vision began to clear and the burning subsided. I found myself in a new unfamiliar place, despite not remembering actually moving anywhere.

Everything seemed darker, even the lights glow dimly. I found myself on an empty road. There were houses that were broken down and collapsing in on themselves. I couldn't see the end of the street in either direction. I walked down the street hoping to find the end or any intersection. It felt like I walked for ever and it seemed as though the houses were repeating. The sky was pitch black with no stars and none of the houses had lights on inside. I decided to turn around and try walking the other direction.

To my surprise, hundreds of mannequins sat facing me. I stared wide eyed at them, I remained completely still. I was waiting for something to happen, for one of them to move. After about ten minutes of facing them down I began to start back down the street, the heads following me as I walked. I felt like I was walking forever but once again there was no end in sight. I wondered how I found myself in this situation, all the things I could have done to avoid this situation.

A loud horn sounded making me jump before I dropped to my knees while covering my ears. I felt like my hands offered no protection from the deafening noise. I knew my ears were ringing but I couldn't even hear them. When the world fell silent all I could hear was the high pitched whine in my head. Once again, I was in a place that I didn't recognize. I now stood on a dirt path with two street lights lighting the way to a well. The mannequin heads lined the path to the well.

They grinned at me. Their lips curled up in an unsettling plastic smile. Their teeth looked real but rotten. Their eyes wide with a crazy gleam.

"Why'd you kill us Carrie? Why?" They spoke in unison. They repeated it over and over again. They got louder every time they recited it. Soon they drowned out the ringing in my ears.

"Shut up! Shut up! Shut up!" I screamed as loud as I could hoping it would make them stop. It only encourages them. I began to stomp on the heads and kick them about, I couldn't take it anymore. I picked a couple up and threw them at the ground as hard as I could, trying to get them to break and shut up. They never shut up.

Hide and Seek

I walked hand in hand with my best friend. I wanted to go to this park, I had seen them setting up some activities that morning while I was on my run. I lived in a small town and he had come to visit from . I made sure to bring him early, so we could see everything they had to offer; The sun was setting on the park. Kids were running around with balloons, glowsticks, and kites. Some of the parents had set up chairs and grills with beers. The park was small, it was a small playscape with 2 slides, a jungle gym and some swings. They also had a playscape for toddlers, which was even shorter than mine. There were tires buried in the sand by the beach. Some kids hopped between them. The water was still, the only waves were small ripples made from the people who were in the water. The kids splashed a play while the adults just sort of stood and chatted, occasionally looking over at their children.

There was a long pier that extended over the water. On the other side of the pier, instead of soft sand, hard jagged rocks rested, keeping people from entering the water on that side. Some of the rocks were large and flat, others were smaller and sharp. I pulled out glow stick jewelry from my bag causing John to chuckle slightly.

"Why do you have glowsticks?" He asked.

"Tradition," I said plainly. I cracked a couple of the glow sticks and handed him a few necklaces and a couple bracelets.

"Why do we need to wear these anyways?" He asked.

"Something about seeing spirits and light protecting you," I said. He rolled his eyes and begrudgingly put the glowsticks on. "There's a hide and seek game with the spirits," I added smiling. "So, we'll be splitting up later to hide," I continued.

"Why are the adults playing, let's just get a beer," He muttered.

"Hey, don't be mean!" I said, playfully elbowing him in the side. "You wouldn't like it if I made fun of your traditions, now would you," I smirked.

"You're right I wouldn't like, but what are we supposed to do, it isn't dark yet," He asked. He looked around. All the shops in the area closed for the festival. People walked around selling glow sticks and others gawked at the sheets hanging from lamp posts.

"We could go look at the activities," I said, trying to encourage him to participate. He followed me over to a table and we looked at the activities. "Want to make ghost lanterns?" I asked.

"We're grown ass adults," he chuckled.

"Grown ass adults can make ghost lanterns," I responded.

"Fine, if you really want to, we can," He stated. I clapped my hands and excitedly giggled before grabbing his hand and dragging him to the area they were setting up for the lanterns. It didn't take too long to make them, he made it a point to make his scary while I made mine cute. When we finished it was almost time for the game. The adults had packed up and rounded up their children.

"Where are you going to hide?" John said.

"I can't tell you," I said, chuckling and playfully pushing his arm.

"Why not?" He was a bit surprised, maybe it was how serious I was taking it or that I possibly didn't trust him with that information.

"The spirits may hear," I whispered in his ear. "It's also cheating," I added a bit louder.

"You sound like you actually believe in this stuff, I thought you weren't superstitious?" He asked.

"I'm not, but there's no harm in playing along for a day," I started swinging our arms playfully. He nodded but I could tell that he was not pleased with me. "Hey, how about we do something that you want to do?" I asked.

"Sounds good," He smiled.

"You have to take it seriously, though," I finished sternly.

We split up so we could scope out good hiding places. The whole town took this festival seriously; it was almost silent, even the kids were quiet. When I found a hiding spot, I made sure to keep it in mind and I continued to wander around trying to spot John until a horn sounded and a countdown from 50 started. People laughed and ran around; even John took off running to his spot. When I returned to my spot I saw two kids huddled there, I felt my stomach twist.

"Three, Two, One... " The water began to glow the most beautiful vibrant blue. I neared it, kneeled down, and touched it. I cupped some of the water and lifted it, but it didn't have the vibrant glow. I began to wade into the water, Soon I was about waist deep into the warm water. I dove down under the surface, the water that was usually dirty, muggy, and disgusting, was crystal clear.

Seaweed danced in the waves and currents while fish darted around aimlessly. They seemed unbothered by me. The sand moved ever so slightly as the water washed over it. The designs are made only by the steady beating of the waves. I reached out and touched a brightly colored fish and it darted away. Something pulled me deeper into the water. I swam further and further into the lake. It seemed as if I could breathe under water. When I stopped, I looked around and the water was still clear, and I saw a glowing figure swim up from the depths. It came face to face with me, we shared eye contact. It swam around me, investigating me, seeing if I was a threat to it or not. It let out a loud howl and I covered my ears. When it stopped I looked around, the water was losing its clear appearance. My lungs burned and I started to swim to the surface. I felt something grab my ankle and try to pull me down as I clawed at the water. Involuntarily my body heaved and gasped for air, my mouth filled with water. I tried coughing and gagging. My vision began to fade in and out. I felt the thing dragging me down. I couldn't fight anymore, I couldn't move. I watched the last of the clear water muddy over before my vision faded to black.

Play Time

I opened a box my friend sent to me. He usually sends me stuff when he comes across creepy or haunted things. Let's make this clear right here, I don't believe in ghosts; I don't believe in spirits or demons. I think that it's all bullshit.

"Fuck," I muttered under my breath as the box cutter sliced open my palm I was using to hold the corner of the box. It wasn't bleeding too bad though, which was good. I went to the bathroom to tend to the wound. After I had it cleaned and bandaged, I returned to the box. When I finally pried the box open, packing peanuts flew everywhere. I tucked my hands blindly into the white Styrofoam mess and pulled out a doll. It had long dark hair. Its eyes were beady and almost colorless, besides the faint shadow of pupils. It wore a black

Victorian style dress that went down to her feet. I rolled up the hem of the skirt and it wore little knee-high socks and black flats.

One thing that was rather strange about the doll is that she carried a little knife. I ran my finger along the edge of the blade. It was a real blade, real metal. Who the hell would give a doll a real knife? It was specially made tiny for the doll. I put her arm down and it swung back up. I went into my supply closet and rummaged around looking for something to replace the blade or at least cover it. I don't want anyone getting hurt thinking that it's a fake knife. I took her to the room I kept all my haunted things and set her on a shelf. When I left, I made sure to lock the door. I know I don't believe in it, but I can't help but try to be safer than sorry. I double check the door before heading to the living room. I sat down on my couch and began reading a book.

I quickly found myself lost in the book, but almost just as quickly I heard some fall to the floor in the other room, causing me to startle. I sat still for a moment, trying to listen for other noises. I felt a strong urge to leave and have someone come back with me, but I felt ridiculous doing that, especially since I knew I was paranoid about the dolls more than a possible break in. I grabbed my phone and creeped down the hall to my room. Taking each step with caution, trying to be silent. I would barely let myself breathe in fear someone, or something would hear me. I shakily checked the closet for anyone despite knowing what room the sound came from. I made my way back to my haunted items room. I found myself hesitant to unlock the door, I'm safe if the door stays locked. I sighed, and just unlocked it.

The door creaked as I opened it. I chuckled when I saw that the doll had fallen over. I quickly put it back on the shelf and made sure it was balancing correctly. I made sure the window was shut and locked before I left the room. There is always this mild thrill when I get a new item, small things suddenly become big things and I get a rush from the unsettled feeling the haunted items bring. I went back into the living room and continued to read my book, this time putting on some music. If anything does happen, I wouldn't be able to hear it, which somehow made me feel safer. I began drifting asleep but I was jolted awake by the sudden silence in the room. I went on my computer; my playlist was manually stopped. I quietly grabbed my phone and got to my feet. I heard a noise coming from the kitchen and I felt my stomach twist.

I quietly rushed to the kitchen only to see my friend looking through my fridge. I grabbed a cup and threw it at him.

"What the fuck!" I shouted. "Why didn't you knock like a normal person, or wake me the fuck up?" I shouted.

"Sorry, I did knock, and I texted you," He replied.

"How did I hear my music turn off but not you knocking?" I asked.

"I didn't turn off your music, it was already off when I got here," he responded, confused.

"Why are you here anyways?" I questioned, changing the subject.

"Well I had nothing better to do with my time," He said tensely, waiting to see if I was going to yell some more. I sighed, no longer being able to feel significantly upset.

"Well I do feel better that you're here, I got a creepy doll today," I explained.

"Oh really?" He asked, chuckling. He was a short guy, almost as short as me. He had shaggy blonde hair and bright green eyes.

"Yeah," I said. "It has a little knife, like a real knife," I added. I grabbed an apple from the fruit pile on the counter.

"Can I see it?" He asked if there was a devious glimmer in his eyes.

"After you're done making whatever the hell you're making," I responded. "I don't want you leaving any food out," I teased. After he finished cooking, we quickly ate and cleaned up. I led him to the room where I kept the haunted items. "Are you ready to shit your pants?" I asked dramatically.

"Gross, but sure," He replied. I unlocked the door and opened it. He walked in, he was obviously shocked by the sheer number of items I had.

"What do you think?" I asked, beaming with pride over my collection. He walked around the room looking at each thing. He touched and fidgeted with some of the items while avoiding others all together.

"Why do you own these?" He asked, his tone was different from his usual playful tone. I Shrugged while I tried finding a better answer.

"They're cool I guess," I replied with mild defeat.

When he got to where the doll carrying a knife was supposed to be I began to freak out. Where the hell did it go? It couldn't have just gotten up and moved. It was a doll. I just silently walked out of the room. I searched the house, all the while my friend kept demanding answers, or at least, for me to say something.

"It moved somehow, I don't know where, I don't know how, but I need to find that fucking doll," I growled.

"Did it wear a little black dress?" He asked.

"Yeah, why? Did you see it?" I questioned harshly. I admit I was a bit frantic.

"It's under your bed," He said, pointing at the doll that was lying on its stomach under the bed. I grabbed it and the gun slid out from under my bed. "You have a fucking gun?" He shouted.

"Yes," I said, kicking it back under the bed. "I have a feeling the doll was trying to get it," I muttered.

"Do you think a doll tried getting your gun?" He asked, I could hear the skepticism in his voice.

"Yes, I know you think I sound crazy, hell, if anyone else was saying what I am saying I would think they're crazy too," I shot. He sighed and shook his head.

"I should probably go," He said, leaving quickly. I took it to the room I kept the other dolls in and set it on the shelf. I turned my back and walked as fast as I could to leave the room. I heard a thud and shuffling. I turned on my heels to see the doll standing in the middle of the room. It was looking right at me and its eyes were different. There was life in its eyes, they were no longer a murky stained marble, they were a brilliant green. I turned around and I heard more shuffling, I turned around and it was closer. I walked backwards out of the room and shut and locked the door. I sat down on my couch trying to figure this out. All my friends would think I'm crazy if I told them about this.

I heard scratching at the door. It sounded like something was dragging a knife on the door. I knew it was that fucking doll. I knew that it was going to try and kill me. I had one of those locks that could only be opened from the outside, but I knew that eventually it'll eventually find a way out. I sighed and marched over to the door. I unlocked it and the doll was standing right there, knife marks in the door. I grabbed it and carried it to my supply closet. I pried the knife from its hands and I tied it up with some paracord.I found a couple stones and blocks and grabbed an old bag I never use and filled it up before putting the doll inside. I put it in the passenger seat and drove to the park. It was a quick drive, only about 3 minutes but it felt like it took forever, I didn't want to be this close to this thing. I walked to the end of the peer and made sure the rope was tight before locking the zippers together.

"Goodbye, you little cunt," I growled. I dropped the bag of rocks into the water and the doll sunk into the murky depths of the water. I went home and I immediately felt safer. I turned on the tv and turned to a kids' channel, I began drifting off once more, the exhaustion of the panic hitting me all at once. When I woke up I knew something was wrong. I immediately shot up, wide awake. I heard movement in my house. The only light in the room was coming from the Tv. I stood up and there was a sharp pain in my arm. I looked down and there was a long cut from the inside of my elbow to my wrist. "What the fuck?" I muttered. I went to the bathroom, making sure to turn on every light. I cleaned the wound and wrapped it in bandages. I was so absorbed in fixing up the cut I didn't notice the doll standing in the doorway. When I did I jumped ten feet in the air. It just stood there staring blankly ahead at the wall. "Mother fucker, how?" I muttered. I grabbed it and marched outside and threw it in the trash can.

I went inside and made sure all my doors and windows were locked before going to bed. I couldn't sleep though. Every time I closed my eyes all I could see was that fucking doll. I sat up and went to the kitchen and started a pot of coffee. I felt like a zombie. Maybe I could put on some cartoons and drift off to sleep with those on. I sat bent over the counter scrolling through my phone when I heard glass break in my bedroom. I rushed in there to see the doll standing on the foot of my bed. It was still dark outside. I growled and grabbed it. I threw it against the wall and began to beat it against the doorframe. Its wooden face getting scuffed and the paint scratching.

"Leave. Me. The Fuck. Alone." I muttered each word over and over again with each hit. I grabbed its head and pulled it from its body. I marched outside and went to my grill. I put the head and body on it and started a fire. I watched the body and cloth burn up. The sizzling of the wood and cloth almost sounded like screams, the scary thing was it was a bit satisfying to hear that sizzle. I didn't leave the grill until there was nothing left of the doll besides ash. When I went inside I laid down and my mind and body finally allowed me to sleep.

Hide

I woke up in a dimly lit room. It was mostly empty. There were a few beat-up chairs, a coffee table, and I was laying on a couch. There were about three other people in the room causing me to jolt up. I scrambled to my feet and whipped my head around checking to see if there were people behind me.

"Who the hell are you?" I panicked. I was nervous and backed myself into a corner. Everyone slowly introduced themselves. There was a tall man who had dark blonde, almost brown hair. He had green eyes and solid features. His name was Andrew. There was a girl who was a little taller than me who had dark skin and short curly hair pulled back into pigtails; her name was Maddy. They were as confused about where we were as I was. The door was locked. It was a solid room that vaguely resembled a class room. There was a loud screech that caused me to cover my ears. When I uncovered them, there was a man talking over a speaker.

"Hello, I'm sure you're all confused, I would be too, but the point of this is very simple, hide from my little... Monster. You live and maybe you'll be able to walk away free," He said with a sinister tone. "I wish you all the best of luck," The man added before we heard a click. The lock on the door unlocked with a thunk and the door swung open. We filed out of the room one by one. We were in a school but it was clearly run down and abandoned. The floor was a mucky yellow, instead of the pristine white. The walls had peeling paint, near the top was stained with dirty water. The tiles in the ceiling were swollen and soggy. Stained by the water. The lockers were rusted, the greenish blue paint was chipping away. There was a strong stench of rot and decay. The sickly-sweet scent invaded my nose; I and everyone else covered their faces.

I walked down the hall. You could hear the echo of our footsteps; the echoes were deafening and disorienting. It was eerie. We roamed through the school trying various doors to rooms and the outside to no avail. I jumped when I heard the piercing sound of a locker opening.

"Oh my god!" I heard Maddy cry out. I spun around and rushed over to the locker. There was the head of a little girl. Her eyes rolled back in her head. A tight, bloody braid curled around the bloody stump of her neck. I felt my stomach rise to my throat and I turned my back to the head. I heard Maddy gagging and retching.

"We should keep going," I whispered out, if I spoke any louder I feared I couldn't hold back my own vomit. I breathed slowly and heavily as we kept moving forward. I froze when I heard a low growl. It almost sounded as if it were distant thunder or a truck hitting a pothole in the distance.

"Hide," I whispered as I ducked into the nearest locker. Closing the door and peering through the slits in it. I heard everyone else scrabble to climb inside lockers. I heard the thumping of heavy footsteps, and the chalky sound of something dragging on the damaged linoleum. My heart was racing in my chest as questions raced through my head. Did I really want to see this thing, what if it finds me, do I really want to be not ready to run for my life? I kept my eyes wide open, my breath caught in my chest. I heard footsteps grow near. I watched a young naked woman come into view, her skin was blue, like she was a corpse. Her hair was long, black, and matted. She was so skinny you could see her bones through her skin, you could easily see her ribs. Her nails were long and dirty. Her hair hung over her face.

I heard a locker door open and slam shut and Andrew rushed over to her.

"Are you okay?" He asked urgently. He tugged his shirt off and forced it into her hands. She stopped walking and just stood absolutely still; she looked like a statue. I couldn't even see her breathe. A low demonic growl escaped her form, a sound belonging to something much larger, and less human than she. Her bones stretched under her skin, jutting out in ways that were just wrong. Her nails grew insanely long, tearing the flesh at the tips of her fingers, exposing bone. Her teeth grew, violently ripping the skin of her cheeks. Her skin was stretched tightly around her bones. In one quick, swift moment, she grabbed Andrew and easily lifted him from the floor. She pulled him into her, biting down on his shoulder. Blood soaked his clothes as his body dangled limply. I heard Maddy's muffled whimper.

She whipped her head around, and looked at the lockers. Her head was turned in an unusual angle. She cocked her head, so it was completely horizontal. You could hear the bones in her neck crack and pop as she did. It stalked over, the creature was looming. She ripped the door open of the locker next to me and the creature dragged Maddy out; Maddy kicked and screamed as she was drugged out of the locker. I looked away and Maddy fell silent with a sickening snap. It took only a few moments to hear slurping and sloshing. I opened my eyes and she looked human again. I closed my eyes before I could look at Andrew and Maddy. I sat there and waited, the sounds of this thing eating was driving me crazy. It felt like forever before it was silent. I opened my eyes and looked through the slots of the locker.

It was gone. My eyes fell to the floor and I felt my stomach churn; there was barely anything left of Andrew and Maddy. I waited for what felt like 20 more minutes. I finaly eased out of the locker, wincing at every crack and pop my bones made as I righted myself. I looked around and I thankfully didn't see the girl, I started trying to scope out possible exits, my eyes fell upon a vent above the lockers. The only problem was being able to get up there silently and by my-self. I would have to climb the lockers and hope for the best. I slowly pulled the locker open. I let out a small sigh of relief when it swung open silently. I climbed the shelves, keeping one hand on the door to help avoid falling down. As soon as I got high enough I started pulling on the vent. I felt the jagged edges of the rusted vent dig into my fingers, but I didn't care at this point. I let out a small yelp as the vent finally popped off.

I heard a heavy thudding of that thing running down the hall-way. There was no way I could make it inside the vent before that thing found me. I decided to climb back into the locker and quickly pulled the door shut, footsteps grew near, I squeezed myself into a tight ball to keep myself from shaking. I didn't want to look out the slits in the locker. I didn't want to risk it noticing me. I clenched my teeth as I heard the deep airy gasps of whatever was on the other side of the door; I feared that it knew I was here. Once again there was a standoff, waiting to see who would move, if either one of us were going to me. I heard the pitter of liquid on the floor right outside my locker. Almost as soon as it came I heard the steps fade off in the other direction.

When all fell silent I climbed out of the locker, my legs felt heavy and my body felt light. I climbed back on top of the locker and made my way into the vent. It was covered in dust and had an even stronger musty smell. I squirmed my way through the vents praying

I would see something that led outside. What used to be cool air now felt exceedingly hot and muggy from my body heat. Every way out of the vents led to a hallway or a classroom. I felt a rising certainty of death, I would be able to stay safe in the vents, but the heat would get unbearable and I would die of dehydration. If I left the vent, whatever that thing was roaming the halls would kill me instead. I sat by a considerably cool vent and ran through all my options, which way would I want to go out, what seemed like the best way to die.

After very little deliberation with myself, I climbed out of the vent silently. A light thud echoed in the halls as I dropped down, I strained my ears to try and hear anything, I was in a section I hadn't yet been in. The halls remained silent and began to stroll down the hallway, the heels of my shoes clicking against the broken tile as I walked. I tried every door that I could see and began using my whole body weight to try and force them open but it wasn't working, they felt as if they were nailed shut, the frames bending under my weight before the doors did. I found myself growing hopeless. Maybe I could find something like a weapon to kill this thing with. I heard the steady thump of its footsteps walking down a nearby hall.

I watched it turn the corner, it instantly saw me. It began to run down the hall with an ear piercing screech. At first it sounded human, then as its bone contorted and changed, her scream sounded more like a demon's howl. Its footsteps grew nearly silent, shifting from a delicate human, to a predator. I was breathing heavily. Adrenaline pulsing through my body. It stopped right before me. I stared up at the thing. Its eyes are bright fiery red. Saliva glistened as it dripped from the oversized teeth, I could see chunks of meat stuck between them. It cocked its head to the left rather than to the right. It seemed confused as to why I wasn't running, screaming, or crying. My eyes burned, I was scared to blink because I knew the second I did I would be a dead girl. Like animals, we were staring each other down. It only took seconds before I felt its claws deep in my stomach and I began to taste blood.

It Brings Death

I sat on my couch playing on my phone while my parents were in the kitchen making themselves coffee. There was the background noise of a show in the background and it was an overall quiet day. A loud silence caused me to jump and my father had dropped his cup of coffee on the floor. My parents shared a look that made me worry because they looked scared. My mother grabbed my hand and we rushed out of the apartment into the hallway, not even bothering to close the door behind us. There was a mob of people in the halls, I couldn't believe all these people lived on the same floor as us and there were some people I didn't even recognize. People looked around murmuring trying to figure out what was going on.

A man approached me and my parents.

"Do you know what happened?" He asked. He had short blonde hair and was clean shaven. He was in his pajamas and was one of the many people I've never seen before. I shook my head and my parents explained that they were just as confused as everyone else here. I peered into someone's apartment that had been left open and he had followed my gaze. There was this thing barely visible through the yellow fog. I could make out long black horns and a long black trench coat; it was floating. I didn't know what I was seeing, I had to be making shapes out of nothing. When the doors opened we rushed inside piling in.

My mother kept her arms around me, we were packed tightly shoulder to shoulder, trying to fit as many people as we could inside. The elevator shook, sending a couple people sprawled out on the floor. I heard a loud and low twang and the elevator began to fall. I clung to the wall for dear life as everyone laid down on the floor. I was pulled down on the floor. I felt at least 3 different people under me. I covered my head and held my breath waiting for the elevator to come to a lethal stop. I heard the metal screeching as it rubbed against itself, but the elevator slowed then suddenly jolted to a stop. I heard glass shatter and felt it raining down on top of me like hail. I looked up and people were groaning, it seemed that everyone was alright. Two people stood and began trying to pry the doors open.

The doors only opened a few inches but it was far enough to see the thing floating down the hallway. I stared in stunned silence waiting for it to notice us. I heard one of the people in the elevator let out an ear piercing scream and the thing stopped and its head turned at an ungodly speed. It didn't have eyes, just hollow sockets where they should be; I felt like it was boring holes through my sole. It had long black horns, it had two long hollow slits where a nose would be, no lips, and it had large, yellow, sharp teeth. It lifted its hand and slowly waved at me. Its long skeletal fingers curled as it slowly cocked his head as if it was now examining the other people in the elevator with me. One of the men jumped up and tried climbing out of the elevator, but before he could even get his legs up the thing grabbed him by the throat and carried him away.

People filed out of the elevator as fast as they could not knowing when or if that thing would come back. When I was pulled out I ran down the stairs and ran outside, the yellow fog was thick and suffocating. I felt like I was spinning in circles when I finally saw it dragging him around a building. I ran around the other side of the building. I tried keeping it in sight while remaining out of its eyeline. It ended up moving into the woods on the outskirts of the town, I had to follow them, I had to know where it was taking him. I tried my best to not make any noise as I continued following it. After what felt like miles it paused, lifting the man higher than before. I grabbed a rock and threw it at the thing hitting it with a sickening splat. It dropped my neighbor who Immediately scrambled to his feet and started running.

"Hey!" I shouted. It turned to face me. "Leave him alone," I said a bit more quietly as I saw its sickening features once more.

"What do you want?" I demanded. I was trying my best not to breathe; the closer it got the more I smelled the scent of rot. It didn't say anything, it just held a sinister grin. I began backing away but within seconds its long fingers wrapped around my throat and lifted me up. I held onto its boney wrist and clenched my teeth, trying to keep calm. It continued on its way. I kicked my legs and clawed at its wrist. Nothing seemed to work. It continued to carry me through the woods and fog.

"Where are you taking me?" I choked out as I continued to struggle against the creature.

"Hell," It croaked in a garbled distorted voice.

"W-Why?" I struggled to speak again. It didn't say anything else. Soon the fog began to clear and I was dropped on the ground. When Ilooked around there were other creatures that looked just like the one before me. It put its hand and pushed me backwards and I started tumbling down a steep drop.

I landed with a hard thump, my body pulsed with pain. I was surrounded by people, some of them looked like we're wasting away and some were trying to crawl up the side of the pit, their fingers bloodied. Other people were dropped down into the same pit as me, I recognized a handful as my neighbors. Many of them began trying to climb out, some of them screamed, and some of them were trying to work in teams to climb out. I just sat down, I waited and watched. I don't know what I was waiting for, but deep down I know I was waiting for something. People sobbed and screamed while others were in panicked frenzies trying to escape the pit. I watched sitting out of reach of the mob. My thoughts drifted away wondering about the people who were turning into savages. Was this what people were at their core? Monster? Selfish beasts that only care about their own survival? It must not be all humans, since I'm just sitting here, not trying to murder and not ripping off ears and fingers.

I gasped as I was easily lifted out of the hole. I looked around frantically. One of those things had pulled me out, it held me firmly in place while other ones dumped a strange, slightly clear, gooey, liquid into the hole. The people cried out in shock, screaming how it burned. I peered down in the hole instantly regretting that decision. I felt my stomach lurch as I watched as their skin bubbled evaporated exposing the fat and muscle underneath. Their eyes seemed to melt from their skulls. I didn't notice one of those things strike a match and drop it in the hole. I jumped back as flames engulfed the pit of people. They screamed and howled in agony as the flames ate them alive. The stench of burning flesh invaded my nostrils. I stared wide eyed down into the bit I was paralyzed in horror. They quickly fell silent, I peered in once more and there was nothing left but dirt.

I looked back at the things and they were still, they stood almost like statues. I wandered through the forest, trying to find my way back out. Stumbling and tripping over stumps and vines. The fog was gone, but I couldn't seem to find my way through this. Nothing looked familiar. Soon I heard shouting and barking. I spun around looking for any sign of life. I wanted to scream, but my body didn't want to. I tried forcing it out, but I couldn't. I spotted some officers with dogs. I stumbled toward them and they saw me. Rushing over and guiding me out of the woods.

Trapped

I looked up at the old apartment building. It was supposed to be abandoned, but somehow, it felt like it was still alive. The building was bowing in on itself, no one lived there for over 40 years. I felt pulled towards the building just as I felt the urge to run away from it. I never had this feeling before. I couldn't bring myself to leave after I had already come so far. I got out of my car and the cool breeze was soothing on my skin. I trudged forward, my feet sinking ever so slightly in the gravel and rocks. I got to the front door and hesitantly pushed it up. The air was warm as it blew past me, a strong odor came with it. The smell of rotting wood and dust caused me to pull my shirt over my nose and mouth. I stepped inside and shut the door gently behind me.

I was increasingly curious about this building, not only because of how long its stood abandoned, but also the stories of how it was haunted and how people would go in and never come out again. There were boards on what few windows there were, I failed to see the point since the front door wasn't even locked. I pulled my flashlight out of my back pocket and shined it on the walls. The paint was peeling off and there was a thick layer of dust all over everything. To my left there was a door with office hours. There was cloudy glass hiding whatever was left in the room. I reached down and the handle was surprisingly cool to the touch despite how warm it was inside. I opened the door and the room was empty. There was carpet on the floor that looked as if it was once white or beige but was now spotted with black and green spots of mold and mildew.

I shined my light around the room quickly making sure there wasn't anything I was missing before backing out of the room. I approached the first apartment on the first floor. I stood staring at the rusted metal that held the apartment number; I reached out and wrapped my fingers around the rusted handle and pushed the door open. The door creaked open, the sound echoed off the walls of the building. The apartment was furnished which took me a bit off guard. The furniture looked weathered and old, but there wasn't any serious damage. The same went with the room, it wasn't falling apart like the office was.

I took a step in and it felt like I was walking against a tarp, almost like I wasn't supposed to enter the room. I wanted to run but I couldn't just turn tail and run, this needed to be explored. I pushed forward, trying to push through whatever was trying to hold me back. When I entered it was overwhelmingly hot. The lights were on and the apartment was now fully decorated. I wanted to investigate the photos on the wall, but I was already over how hot it was in the room; I began to pant just standing still. I backed out of the room and I let out a sigh of relief when the cool, damp air met with my skin. I rested my hands on my knees and allowed myself to take a long deep breath of the cool air. When I looked up the room was rotted away like the others, the furniture that, seconds ago, pristine, looked like burned piles of ash.

I had conflicted feelings, I wanted to keep investigating, but I also wanted to go home and forget what just happened. What just happened? Why did that just happen? Why did this just happen to me? The more questions I had the more I wanted to stay and investigate. I opened the door of the apartment immediately next door, letting out a sigh of relief when it was decrepit. I went from door to door, each one of them eerily similar to the last. I finally moved to the second floor. When I opened the first door on the floor, it was like the first apartment. It looked like this place was still occupied, the walls were a bright beautiful golden yellow. The floor was freshly polished wood. The hallway was dotted with tables with plastic plants resting on them. At the very end was a large bay window with a dark wood frame.

I glanced behind me to the dark colorless walls of the stairway, everything painted with gross shades of Gray, Green, and Blue. I stepped into the beautiful golden hallway, this experience wasn't like before, there was no force trying to keep me out. I felt almost lighter stepping through the doorway. The temperature stayed the same. I took a few steps into the hallway before the door to the stairwell slammed shut. I let out a loud shriek as it made a loud clanging noise. I spun on my heels and ripped the heavy door open. I gasped in horror, the stairs were gone, in its place was a hallway that was an exact mirror of this one. My heart began to race. Was I trapped here? I should have left when I had the chance. I should have never entered this building. Am I going to die here? Then it hit me, I grabbed the plant off the nearest table and drug it over to the window on the far end of the hall. I looked down and saw my car parked several yards away.

I braced myself as I rose the table over my head and threw it against the window. I heard shattering of glass and the table passed through the window, but it still looked intact. I shakily reached my hand out to touch the glass and my hand was stopped by the cool material. I retreated quickly and stumbled backwards. I turned around and ran to the door and pulled it open, it was still a mirror of the hallway, but the table and planter were still in their original positions. I ran to the other side of the hall, to the window. I looked down and in horror I saw my car parked. I took a deep breath before slamming my elbow into the glass. It stopped dead in its tracks. Damn. I walked back to the door and opened it. The same yellow hallway. What am I supposed to do? What does the building want? I walked stiffly to the bay window and sat on the cool wood. I needed to think.

I was too scared to open any of the doors in fear of seeing something other than this weird vision. If I don't, I could be stuck here forever. In classic horror stories everything is supposed to end at sunrise. I waited for a few minutes to let my heart calm down and to build up my bravery so I could open each one of these apartments and find a way to leave this hell hole and never return. After a few moments I forced myself to my feet. My knees shook violently, they threatened to give out. I walked over to the door closest to me. It was on the left-hand side. The door was tall and made out of a dark wood, similar to the window pane. I wrapped my fingers around the cool golden handle. I pushed the door open and the inside was decayed like the rest of the building.

I stepped inside and closed the door behind me. I walked through the rubble. I looked around, somehow seeing this place decayed and not perfectly pristine like the hallway. I walked over to the window. It was boarded up; I knew that I was nowhere near strong enough to pull them off the window. I went into the bathroom. The faucets were rusted and covered in grime. I moved to the bedroom. It was a lot like the front room. I went back to the door; my heart was racing in anticipation and fear. I wrapped my fingers around the handle once more and pulled the door open. I almost cried when I saw the same golden hallway. I left, but I left the door open. I went to and from different apartments and each of them were like the last.

As I entered a random room the door slammed shut behind me, causing me to let out a yelp. I rushed forward and tried opening it but the handle wasn't moving. I turned around and pressed my back against the warm wood. My eyes darted around the room finding there was nothing off with the room. It was perfectly normal, too normal. I took a few steps into the room and that's when I heard it.

It started off sounding like a tea whistle. The farther I stepped into the room the more it seemed to morph into a woman's scream. I tried hunting the sound down. I couldn't seem to find the source of the sound. It got louder and louder, I had to cover my ears because it had grown painful. Just as suddenly as it started it just fell silent. I stood up disoriented. It went from deafening loud to a deafening silence. I began to smell gas and I tripped on a rug and almost like a flash everything was back to rotting wood. I stumbled to my feet and ran out of the room. I pulled a door open and stumbled out but I paused when I saw a golden door.

Everything inside me was screaming to not go up to it. Screaming for me to just leave, I was drawn to the door though. It was radiating warmth. There were intricate curling designs with little leaves and doves on the frame. I pulled the door open and gazed into the room that was flaming. There was a woman in the flames, it wasn't the flames making a woman burn alive in the flames. I stared blank, in shock. She was reaching out to me. Beckoning me into the flames. I wanted to turn on my heels and run but my feet felt like they weighed a million pounds. I felt my hand lifting up, reaching out to take her hand in mine. I felt her fingers wrap around my wrist and I felt my body jerk forward into the flames.

The Storm

I woke up, I rubbed the sleep out of my eyes and I got up. I pulled on my clothes and made my way to the living room. I turned on the TV and went to the kitchen to make myself some breakfast. The weather man was ranting about some unique weather we never had before. There was a Tornado warning but I didn't really listen to it. I live in a major city and Tornadoes almost never hit major cities. So, it most likely won't happen. I finished eating and I did the dishes and checked my phone. I had a text from my boyfriend wanting to meet me in the social room on the roof. Pulling on my sneakers I replied to his text letting him know I was on my way up.

I went into the hallway and locked the door behind myself. I walked over to the elevator and pressed the button, it didn't light up, I pressed it more aggressively and sighed angrily when it remained dim. I walked to the stairwell and made the long march up to the roof. I pulled the door open and walked out onto the covered patio. The roof had a glass covering that protected the patio from the elements. I saw him sitting at one of the little wooden tables right next to one of the windows. It was cloudy outside. The clouds were so thick that the world was tinted a light, soft blue. I sat down next to Alex and he smiled at me.

"Did you hear the news this morning?" He asked.

"About the Tornado warning or something else?" I groaned, resting my head on the cool table. Alex let out a small chuckle. Alex was tall and had shaggy shoulder length black hair. He had brown eyes that you could get lost in.

"The Tornado, it's supposed to be landing on the other side of the river and lucky us we have a perfect view ," Alex said smiling pointing out the window that was dotted in raindrops.

"There isn't going to be a tornado," I replied.

"Why do you say that?" He asked, raising an eyebrow.

"We live in a city," I said shrugging. He remained silent and just stared out the window.

"I mean if a tornado lands we'll see it, if not, we get to spend time together which will be nice," He said smiling. I couldn't help but smile too and place a small peck on his lips. He smiled and looked down at his lap. I studied the other side of the river. It was calm like every other morning, I looked up at the sky.

The sky was blanketed in dark clouds, they were churning and moving into itself. To be honest, it kind of scared me, it's been so long since I've seen a storm that bad. The sky was flashing with bright light and thunder rumbled through the room. There were a handful of other people up here with us, they were watching the sky like us. I was hypnotized by the way the clouds curled around themselves, merging, mixing, and churning. Across the river, I saw a funnel form, just a small bump forming at the bottom of a cloud. It slowly began to stretch like taffy, pulling itself towards the ground. I felt my heart begin to thump in my chest. It was a drum in my ear. I watched as it began to bounce on the ground, throwing up dirt and debris. I grabbed Alex's hand.

"We have to go," I murmured, pulling him out of the lounge room.

"Why?" He asked. He seemed genuinely confused. "I thought you liked tornadoes," He stated.

"It touched down, we shouldn't be up here," I said, pulling him to the elevator. I pressed the button frantically. "Is it really shut down?" I muttered to myself. I pulled him out of the elevator and ran for the stairs. He finally slid from my grasp and followed me down the stairs. Our footsteps echoing in the narrow damp space. Every other floor had a window, thankfully looking at the river. I couldn't help but glance out the window every time I passed. The Tornado was getting larger and getting more violent. It was nearing the river. Hurling items into the water, huge waves exploding outward.

"Go, go, go!" I shouted. I noticed a few other people were heading for the basement as well. When we entered, I slammed the door shut, before sitting on the floor next to the door. "So, did you guys see how big it was getting?" I asked panting.

"Well we're safe now," a woman I didn't recognize said.

"The lower we get the better," I murmured. I began to roam about the basement, I've only been down here once. I opened the doors and peered in.

"Hey I found a ladder!" A person shouted from the other side of the basement. I spun on my heels and walked towards the voice. A person was crouched down in front of a ladder leading down into a dark hole in the ground.

"Who's going first?" I asked. I looked around the group of strangers. I jumped when the basement door opened and closed with a loud screech and a bang. I left the room I was called into to see yet another group of people entering the basement.

"Do you guys know how close the tornado is?" I asked.

"It's about halfway across the water now, more people are coming down," A girl responded. I looked around. There were still a lot more people that could be down here comfortably.

"I'm going to go check the first few floors to see if there are other people left that need help," I stated. Sirens began to wail. I made my way up the stairs to the first floor and began knocking on every door I could. People coming out confused. The sirens must have woke them up. I Sent them to the basement and made my way to the second floor, the building shook and the lights went out. I heard tons of screams and debris fell through the stairs. I looked up and there was a huge chunk of the wall missing. I continued my way up. My heart pounding in fear, the wind howled as rain poured through the hole.

I entered the second story and repeated what I did on the first floor. A deafening sound of metal crunching and rocks falling apart floored me as a large piece of debris was sent through the second floor. The rain was still falling heavy. I didn't risk going higher, the tornado was already launching debris at the building. I followed the group of people down. As we descended, I noticed water running down the stairs. Once we hit the basement level, we were knee deep in water. I went to the room with the ladder, thankfully it was elevated so the water was just now dribbling down. I climbed down first helping the other get down. I looked around taking in the small room that seemed to be hidden, it was an electrical room. I felt my nerves instantly rise.

"You okay?" Alex asked. I wrapped my arms around him tightly. "I'm fine, just scared," I responded. I heard a thud against the door. People were pleading for help to be let in. Then I heard a blood curdling scream. I started climbing up the ladder, feeling the need to help these people.

I opened the door which was hard with all the water putting pressure on it and I screamed as a corpse floated in. It was missing a head; you could see remnants of the skull and spine still attached clinging to each other by the little bit of flesh, muscle, and tissue that remained. I stumbled backwards falling down. The body floated towards me and I struggled to crawl backwards, desperate not to be touched by it. I was finally helped up, and that's when I saw it, more body's tumbled and were carried by the water down. I was gasping for air at this point. I couldn't breathe, my ears were ringing. I forgot where I was going. Until I was grabbed and led back to the ladder. I fumbled and slipped as I climbed down. Eventually falling and scraping my hand on the concrete floor. I was helped up by Alex and a few of the strangers. I looked up, the water stopped flowing clear and flowed a sick orange red.

I watched as the body slid more and more over the edge. I backed myself against the wall. I couldn't take my eyes off the corpse. I screamed as the building shook again, sending the body tumbling along with a couple others. A few of the bodies landed on some of the others in this pit. A few of the others began to scream as well. The bodies laid in the small pool of bloodied water. The wind's howling got louder and louder. The entire building and the foundation creaked and groaned as the tornado placed strain in the building. I heard the heart stopping sound of concrete ripped from the building. Looking up I could see the concrete ceiling of the basement was cracked and crumbling. The scream of metal being stretched and torn was heart stopping.

Soon it all stopped. We all looked at each other in confusion. It was silent, no wind, no building creaking. I took the first steps up. The echo of my footsteps echoed in my ears. I went to the basement door and tugged it open. My stomach dropped at what I saw. Bodies littered what was left of the stairway. I climbed what was left of the stairs, nothing existed after the third floor. I entered the door to the third floor, the apartments were torn apart, dead bodies were once again strewn across the floor, over walls. I felt dizzy, like I couldn't breathe. I rested my hands on my knees and gasped for air, my nose filling with the smell of blood. I gagged on the smell. I gagged at the sight, until I just fell over, my vision fading in and out before I just gave in.

The girl by the River

I worked alone at night, it happened more often than I liked. It seemed like every time I worked a night shift alone; I'd see a girl walking by the river across the street. I don't know if she was always there when I was alone, but she creeped me out. The way she walked seemed so unnatural, it was stiff and jerky. One night I was working alone. It was getting close to fall, so the night was fairly chilly. I once again saw the girl, she wore a long night gown that came just past her knees. He long black her whipped in the wind. There was part of me that wanted to invite her inside for the night, so she wouldn't be cold.

I watched her as I did my duties. Cleaning the windows and emptying waste baskets. I began to notice, it seemed as if she was getting closer. I could make out more of her features than before. She moved more unnaturally than I initially thought. Her arms and legs bent and shifted in abnormal ways, ways that would be impossible for a normal person to move. I felt my heart racing. I felt scared and uneasy. I kept going about my job, all the doors and windows were locked. I still felt ill-at-ease, looking up every so often to make sure she wasn't outside the window looking at me. It seemed like every time I looked up; she was just a little bit closer than before. I didn't feel safe. I called a close friend of mine to come up to my job and wait outside for me to finish then take me home.

He wouldn't be able to come until 20 minutes after my shift, I didn't care, I was going to wait that 20 minutes. I finally moved to the back. I felt safe, out of sight out of mind, there was a part of me that feared her being there when I went back out to the front. I cleaned, scrubbed, and organized, and the fatal time came when I had to go up to the front. I didn't have access to the cameras so I couldn't even check from the back. I kept telling myself that the doors and windows were locked so even if she was there, she couldn't hurt me, and that I was safe, but deep down, I felt a pit of dread in my stomach. I stepped out of the back, not even looking at the window. I did everything in my power to not look at the window. I heard a bone chilling scratching. It was slow and long and sounded like when you glide scissors through wrapping paper.

Against everything in my body. I slowly lifted my eyes to the window to see the woman standing there, dragging her nails down the window, staring at me with pure hatred and anger. She was easily 7 feet tall. She was a sickly blue color. He black hair is greasy like she hasn't washed it in years. Her bones jutted out at unnatural angles. Her nails were long and unkept. I jumped and yelped when she slammed on the window.

"LET ME IN!" She howled. Her voice was inhuman. It boomed and shook the windows. It was almost like a low dog growl. I couldn't help but stare, frozen in horror. Unsure of what to do or how to respond. I ran into the back and grabbed my phone. I called the police but the phone just kept ringing. No operator, no one. Just the steady ring. I called my friend, crying and screaming, pleading for him to please just come, finally he broke down and promised he'd be there in ten minutes.

I took a deep breath as I tried to convince myself to go out. I didn't know what was worse, seeing her and being able to calculate her next move, or not seeing her but not knowing what she was doing or where she was at. I heard her tapping the windows. The same way you roll your fingers against a desk when you click the rapid click of nails against the glass, a split pause then the roll of nails again. The grew fainter and louder, almost as if she was moving around.

"I won't hurt you!" She sang loudly. Her voice was different, it was shrill and high. It sounded like two women's voices were meld together and put through a fan on low.

I cracked the door separating the back from the front, not so much that it was noticeable but so much that I could see. I saw her slowly walking back and forth. Her bones seemed to crack and dislocate with every move. She wasn't human. I knew that for sure. She stopped. Did she see me? I quickly shut the door. I wanted to keep looking, I wanted to know where she was. I didn't want to risk losing sight of her. I heard loud bangs, she must be hitting the windows again. I once again opened the door just a crack. She was slamming her head against the glass. I stared wide eyed, frightened.

"LET! ME! IN!" Saying each word each time she hit the glass. Soon blood was visible on the glass and I wanted to scream when I saw the glass beginning to crack. Spider-webbing out more and more each time she made contact.

Just as the glass began to sink inwards, almost as a saving grace, my friend sped into the parking lot, getting out of his car with a gun. The woman ran away. It was more of a quick hobble. She ran into the darkness, moving in that inhuman way. I ran out to my friend, sobbing. I was terrified. I locked up the store even though I wasn't done. I went home and I never returned. Though sometimes when I look out my window at home, I think I see her in the distance, walking.

Mutant

I sat in my friend's car; we were outside an old nuclear plant. The facility was surrounded with barbed wire; we were going to break in and see what it was like inside. What the bowels of this place looked like. I looked at my best friend, Liz, she could see how anxious I was. I pulled my short hair back into a half ponytail and contemplated what we should do once we got inside. We got out of the car and shut our doors at the same time. We gawked at the huge building that stood before us.

"What do you think we'll find in there?" Liz asked. I shrugged.

"How do you think we're going to get in there?" I asked. She pulled out wire-cutters.

"We're going to be the first," She grinned as she sipped the wire cutters. I eagerly followed her over the fence and I watched as she clipped away at the fence; I looked around making sure no one was watching us or even saw us.

Soon she was peeling back the fence, holding it open for me to go first. I eagerly climbed through the waist height hole in the fence. When I stood up I pulled the fence through my side and held it open for her to climb through as well. We couldn't help but grin at each other as she made it out the other side of the fence. We quickly made our way to the building, wanting to get inside and out of site.

After about 15 minutes of walking we finally made it to the plant, it looked so much taller than when we parked the car.

"I'm happy to know there are no landmines," I joked as we walked around the outside of the building. Broken cement crunch and cluttered as we walked. "What do you think is there?" I asked.

"I just think we'll find some old paperwork, and if we're really lucky we might find someone," she responded.

"I hope not," I shot back, my voice came out more shrill than I was hoping.

We paused when we reached the door, building the tension we were grinning at each other at this point. Hearts racing, making memories to one day tell our kids. I grabbed the handle and tugged, I let out a low grunt when the door wouldn't move. We looked at each other a bit disappointed.

"So, what do we do now?" I asked. She ignored the question and tried the door as well, but it didn't budge. She looked around and her face lit up. Off to the side of the building. There were windows, I guess it was an office section or a break room area for the employees. I followed her over. She wrapped her sweatshirt around her elbow.

"Let's hope there's no alarms. If there is, make a beeline for the car," She said. She slammed her elbow against the glass and it shattered. I let out a sigh of relief when the night remained silent. She used her hoodie to clean up the glass around the edge of the window, leaving just a hollow frame.

"Give me a boost," She demanded. I knelt down and interlocked my fingers and she stepped on my hands and I pushed her through the window. I heard the glass scraping against the concrete and she leaned out the window to help me through. I stumbled on my landing and fell, thankfully not cutting myself in the process.

"Where in," I said anxiously, rubbing my hands on the sides of my thighs. My eyes darted everywhere, trying to take in every detail of the room through the darkness. We looked around the room and it was set up like a small office. Bookshelves built into the walls. It was surprisingly untouched and clean for a building so old, maybe given it's an old power plant with barbed wire they thought they'd have security in this place. There was a thick layer of dust all over the ground, our steps left clear and defined prints, we really were the first people to enter since it shut down.

"This is pretty boring," She groaned.

"It's just one room in this entire plant, save judgements until at least half way through this adventure," I replied. "But this room is pretty dull," I admitted. We walked out of the room revealing a short hall with doors evenly spaced apart. "Which door?" I asked.

"Why not all of them; we do have all night," Liz responded. One by one we opened doors each creaking and reverberating through the halls. Looking behind us, I noticed something off. The dust has been shifted, like something was being drug across the ground.

"Liz," I whispered. I nudged her and pointed at the fresh marks in the dust. It led from one of the rooms that we have yet to go into a door at the end of the hall the hung slightly ajar. She chuckled slightly. "Liz, this isn't a laughing matter," I hissed quietly.

"It's probably an overfed animal or something," She replied laughing. "You look like you're about to piss yourself," She continued. I felt my face grow red out of anger. "Oh, come on, I'm sure it's nothing seriously dangerous," She assured me, trying to make me feel better. "Let's follow it to show you it's nothing to be scared of," She said, grabbing my hand and leading me down the hall after the long line of displaced dust. I let her lead me towards the door, my heart racing in fear. There was just another long streak leading to another door. I refused to go any further, I was not going to go into the maw of this place trying to find something that may or may not be some wild animal.

"Liz, let's just go home, I don't know if I want to see what this is," I whispered out. My voice shook and I was trying to free my hand from hers.

"It's going to be fine, I promise," She seemed more angry than sympathetic now.

"Come on, what if it's dangerous?" I asked.

"Don't you think it would have attacked us if it was?" She asked. She made a valid point. I hesitantly followed her, I still felt uneasy, I felt like I was holding my breath as we followed the trail. As we got closer a smile grew on her face, she looked excited and she held my hand even tighter, refusing to let me pull away. We finally reached the second door, once more it was cracked open. With one swift kick and loud boom made my heart skip a beat. The door slammed wide open, slamming against the concrete wall.

"See, nothing, let's go home." I insisted. I finally managed to free myself from her grasp and started running back to where we came. I heard a second pair of footsteps behind mine, she was really chasing me. I finally got back to the window and I began to try and climb out in the process cutting myself on a stray piece of glass.

"Shit!" I hissed looking at the oozing cut. Blood quickly ran down my arm. My friend entered the room and she stopped; we were both breathing heavily. Chests heaving.

"Look what you did," She shot.

"You're the one that wouldn't let me leave!" I shouted.

"Why are you so afraid, you always play those scary games!" She yelled. Our voices were booming in the empty room.

"I'm not crazy for a suicide mission that's why I ran, we didn't know what that thing was, it could be dangerous" I responded simply. I wasn't going to have this fight, not now. "I'm going to the car," I responded. I jumped out the window and made my way to the car. When I got to the car I waited on the hood, looking at the window we snuck in through. The longer I waited the angrier I got, but after even longer, it shifted to concern.

Just as I was getting out of the car, I heard a loud sharp scream that was almost immediately cut off. I began running towards the building, the worst case playing through my mind, I ran in there and she was brutally murdered. I eagerly climbed back into the window the second I got inside I ran down the halls following the footsteps in the dust. I kept thinking about how I should have never left her alone, and how it was all my fault. I kept following the steps down flights of stairs, not realizing I was also following the other trail. I flew through one of the doors in the basement then I saw it. It looked like two people joined at the torso. Not like conjoined twins, but more like the bottom half of two people were cut off and both the top halves were sewn together at the seam. They were covered in blood and I saw Liz's mauled body on the floor.

Their joints bent in odd angles. While one ends arms bent like a normal human; the other side bent in the wrong way. Their necks were oddly elongated, as if someone grabbed their head and pulled as hard as they could and stopped just short of ripping their flesh. Their skin twisted around itself. It was loose in some places and tight in others. Their faces were like a mummy's. It was dry, flakey, and tight. They had no eyes, just shallow holes where their eyes should be. Their noses were half decayed away, they had sharp disgusting teeth almost as if they were ripped from a dog's mouth and forced into theirs. The one that was trying to crawl away began to wail and howl. The one eating Liz's insides immediately looked towards me. I snarled and began to claw and fight its way towards me. Dragging the howling one behind it.

I bolted for the outside tripping and falling in the process. I couldn't think straight. I heard it behind me, but I wasn't going to risk looking behind me. I turned a corner attempting to lose it. I found myself twisting and turning through rooms. Then I ran into a dead end. I heard the thing moaning and howling. I looked around the room I was in and spotted a few large empty boxes. If they were a little larger, I would have been able to fit inside. I crouched behind them. I mentally cursed at myself, that thing could follow me right into this room and to my hiding place from my footprints in the dust. The noises the thing made grew closer. I was forging a plan hoping it would stick to my footsteps and I could bolt for the door and maybe lock it into one of the many rooms I ran through. Then I heard the faint sound of flesh against concrete. A long dragging noise then silence, long dragging noise, silence. I held my breath, waiting and listening to the sounds getting louder and louder. I finally heard it entering the room.

Suddenly out of nowhere the boxes went flying, I yelped and fell on my ass, before I scooted myself against the wall and stared at the thing. It started right back at me. Blood stained its mouth. I was almost certain I was going to die. I couldn't feel my legs. It made its way over to me. I pressed myself against the wall, part of me was hoping I would phase through the wall, or wake up. It brought its face within inches of mine. I could smell the blood on its breath. It had its lips pulled back, showing me its teeth. My heart was in my stomach, I felt like I was seconds from vomiting. The other, more submissive end began to howl and weep. The side facing me backed away and left the room. I watched as it dragged itself away from me. After it left the room, I felt my chest burning. I forgot to breathe. I let go of the breath I was holding and gasped for air. The second I went to breathe out I threw up all the contents in my stomach.

After I finished throwing up, I sprinted for the exit, hoping to never see that creature again. I ran to the car and floored it home. Why did it spare me, why didn't it eat me like it did Liz? What was I going to tell the cops, what am I going to tell our friends? My mind was still spinning, I don't think I could get far enough away from that building. I don't think I could feel safe knowing that thing is in there, alive. Sometimes I consider going back, with a gun or something, and killing it.

Why I'm Scared of Playhouses

I never liked those playhouses that they had in Fast Food restaurants. I don't know why, but they make me uneasy. When I was a kid my parents took me to the largest playhouse in the state for my birthday, I wasn't a very social kid. I preferred my isolation. When we got there, I immediately knew what was up. Hard to miss the humongous glass room encasing a towering playhouse.

"We're here sweetie!" My mom cheered happily from the front seat. I looked at the building and I wasn't too excited. It was obvious by the lack of a smile on my face.

"You don't like it?" My dad said, he sounded as if he was upset

"I do," I trailed off. We got out of the car, I eyed the glass room, kids running around and laughing. We walked inside, we ordered, and made our way to the playscape. We sat down in the corner of the room; I took my time eating, being very intentional. It towered over us, it was larger than a small apartment.

When I finished eating my mom shooed me into the playscape, I kicked off my shoes and made my way to the entrance. There was a sinking pit of dread in my stomach. I took my first steps inside. When inside it, it was almost like I was in a whole different world, it's crazy, the mind of a child, a few steps can change your whole perception of something. I began to climb; how high did this go? I had a sudden wave of realization rush over me. I didn't see any other kids, the place was crawling with them before I entered, but now I'm absolutely alone. I found my way to the tube tunnels, bright orange, they were built like a maze. Images of lost children flashed across my mind, being lost and needing help and no one being able to because they were too high up.

I crawled through, the neon orange hurt my eyes and I just wanted to lay in the mesh netting and close my eyes, pretend I was at home, reading. I finally found my way out of the tube maze into a blue hard plastic section. I thought I saw a kid go down a slide. I crawled over. The slide was bright red, I pushed myself down the slide. The plastic stuck to my legs. When I reached the bottom the room was filled with foam mats. I went into a netted section; I couldn't walk straight. Why weren't there any other kids? There were so many before I came in here, how have I not talked to one? I found my way to another tube maze, this one in yellow, or was it the same section and I thought it was orange? I climbed inside and a sickly stench hit my nose. I contemplated going through or just climbing down to the ground floor and just told my parents that I didn't want to be here and wanted to go home. I took a big breath and held it as I crawled through. I took small breaths to avoid smelling whatever it was.

It sort-of smelled like old food in the trash can. I crawled through the turns and loops. I saw an orange glow from another tube. I crawled down and noticed something, it was reflecting red, it wasn't orange. I sped up.

"Hello!" I shouted I was relieved to see another kid, at this point I would rather talk to someone than be alone. There was no response, no movement, I felt that moment of safety fade away. I rounded the corner and quickly began to scoot backwards. I gasped for air, it felt like suddenly all the oxygen was gone. All I saw was blood; there wasn't a person, just a puddle. I began to try and find my way out. I forgot the route that I took in here. I began to crawl through random tunnels, I felt my heart racing. I rounded a corner and once again I saw the blood puddle. Was it the same puddle, was it a different one? I turned around and took another route back. The tubes began to look more orange than yellow. It was a slow but steady shift.

Minutes past the tubes grew darker, and as they grew darker, they grew softer. What was once hard industrial plastic felt more like foam now. It felt like they were growing warm. I felt myself begin to sweat. It was getting hard to breathe. It began to shift from orange to red. What was going on? It felt like the tubes were getting stickier as they got softer. I noticed my hands were covered in a thick red liquid. It was sticky and congealed. I smelled it and it smelled like metal. I didn't crawl in anything though. It looked like the walls were pulsating, breathing, moving. Was this place alive? As I crawled looking for an escape the tube felt like it was getting smaller and smaller. Encasing me in it. It began to develop the texture of meat. Every time I moved; I heard a squelch. Then it hit me. Is this alive, or am I losing my mind?

I Sighed and just laid on the bottom of the tube. I couldn't keep going. I was covered in sweat. I was panting, it felt like it was a million degrees. The tube has gotten so small I could barely move. My vision began to blur. I felt sticky and slimy from the red gunk covering my body. It felt like a weight on my chest. I don't remember anything after that. The doctors say that it was a stressed induced hallucination, but I've never felt the same about those play houses since. I've been absolutely terrified of them since that day.

The Killer Side Job

It was a slow day at work and I stood at the hostess stand playing on my phone when it started ringing at max volume making me jump. One of the waitresses I worked with jumped as well. I had a job after work, she was a kind old lady. She had a cat; it was a little asshole and I barely saw it while I was cat sitting. It was basically getting paid to watch tv, I cat-sit so much I have a key to her apartment. After work I got in my car, and pulled out of the parking lot, it was still fairly light outside, the sun was just going down. She only lived a few minutes down the road. I pulled into her parking lot, and only about 4 other cars sat in the lot. I got out and locked my car. I made my way to the door. I knocked before putting my key in the lock and let myself in. As soon as I stepped inside a horrendous smell hit my nose. I pulled my shirt over my nose. It didn't help.

"Mrs. Brighte?" I shouted into the apartment. I made my way into the kitchen, dishes sat in the sink, mold growing on some. I felt a pit grow in my stomach. I jumped when I felt something brush my leg. I looked down and her cat looked skinny, it was usually a fat cat, I looked over at its food bowl and water bowl. Both empty, I grabbed its food and poured it into the bowl, I grabbed its water bowl and filled it up with the bottle of water in my purse. I set it down as well and the cat rushed to the bowls. "Mrs. Brighte!" I shouted once again, this time my voice was shrill with worry. I moved to the dining room. The fruit in her fruit bowl were shriveled and rotten, fruit flies buzzing around in clouds. I made my way to the living room and the TV was on. I turned the TV off. I went to the final room, her bedroom. I held my breath as I slowly opened the door.

I gasped when I saw her laying on her bed, there was blood everywhere. I ran out of the room, out of the apartment, and doubled over outside the door throwing up the dinner I had at work. I pulled out my phone and shakily dialed 9-1-1. I held the phone to my ear as it rang.

"9-1-1, what's your emergency?"

"I'd like to report a murder, I came to cat sit for a client and I let myself in and found her in her room dead, I think it happened a while ago,"

"What's your location?" She asked. I told her where I was and after about 10 minutes three cop cars pulled up. The officers introduced themselves and asked me a few questions, an ambulance pulled up and wheeled a gurney out. I watched as the officers talked into their walkie talkies, I saw them wheel out a stretcher covered in a black tarp. An officer walked over to me.

"You're free to go home, we'll keep in touch," He said.

"Can I bring the cat with me? She doesn't have any family, I'd hate for it to go into a shelter," I asked. He called another officer over and they had a small whispered conversation. The officer he called over nodded and walked away.

"It's fine," He said. I went to walk up to the apartment, but he stopped me. "My partner is getting it," He said firmly. I nodded and waited patiently. His partner came out with the cat in his arms. He handed it to me and I went to my car and put it in the back seat, I got in the driver's side and looked in the mirror. I noticed something staring at me from the other side of the parking lot, I couldn't make out, if it was a person or a shadow. When I got to my apartment, I turned my car off and noticed something off, it was a shadow, it looked like a man.

I spun around hoping to see what it was, but when I looked it was gone. I shrugged it off, I think I'm just stressed, I just saw my longtime client butchered. I picked up the cat and got out of the car, closing it with my hip and making my way inside, making sure to lock the door behind me. I set the cat down and got two bowls out of my cupboard and set them down, I found some cat nibble in the cabinet and poured some into one bowl and poured water into the other. I felt so bad for that cat. I went into the living room and turned on the TV before returning to the kitchen and getting a Soda out of the fridge before sitting down at the table and scrolling through my phone. I jumped when I saw something walk past my window out of the corner of my eye.

I got up and walked over, looking out. There didn't seem to be anyone around who could have walked past my window. I saw a neighbor smoking on her porch, some kids playing in the yard across the street, and a couple deep into a make out session on the hood of an old beat up sports car. I sighed and shut the blinds, maybe it's my imagination. I yelped as my phone began to ring, it was an unknown number. I declined it. My phone began to ring again, and it occurred to me it could be the officers so I picked up.

"Hello?" I asked

"Did you like it?" A strange, unsettling voice asked.

"What?" I was confused, I felt my stomach creeping up into my throat, something was wrong.

"I did it for you," He said, breathing heavily.

"Did what?" I asked, I didn't want to think that he killed that poor old woman, for me. I grabbed a pad and paper, and quickly wrote down the number.

"I killed her for you," He said before hanging up.

I broke out in a cold sweat. I pulled out the card the officer handed me and shakily dialed his number.

"Hello, officer Rolf speaking," He said in a very monotone voice.

"Hi, you gave me your card earlier today, a man just called saying he killed her, for me, I don't feel safe, I wrote down the number if that's any help," I said, my voice wavered.

"The number will be very useful; I'll be right there, make sure your doors and windows are locked, will you give me your address?" He said, his voice was firm and it made me feel slightly better. I told him my address and the number before I went around the apartment making sure the windows and doors were locked like he said. I sat in the living room trying to focus on the program on the TV trying not to think about this whole situation. I let out a short scream when someone pounded on the door. I walked over to the door slowly.

"W-Who's there?" I called out; my voice shook so hard.

"It's Officer Rolf and Officer King!" He shouted through the door. I looked through the peephole and hastily opened the door for them and locked it as soon as they both were inside. "I brought officer Kon with me because I thought you'd feel better with a female officer with us,"

"Did you track the number; do you know who did it?" I asked eagerly.

"Our specialists are working on tracking the number, it was very smart of you to write it down," Officer Kon assured me. "Officer Rolf is going outside keeping an eye on the apartment and I'm going to stay in here with you," She said, smiling at me softly. It was very comforting.

Officers kept an eye on my apartment for about a week, and continued to do random check-ins. I began to feel safer, I went back to work and I appreciated the normality my life was beginning to go back to. I was standing at my podium and waiting for the customers. It was still slow, scrolling through my phone before my phone began to ring. It was an unknown number, it wasn't the officers, and it wasn't the phone number that called me telling me they killed that sweet old lady for me. I hit the answer.

"Why did you go to the police, don't you like what I did for you?" A voice asked. I gasped and my phone slipped from my grip. It clattered to the floor. My heart was racing and I felt sick to my stomach. I bent down and scrambled to pick up my phone. I put it to my ear but the person already hung up and I dialed Officer Rolf's number.

"Officer Rolf speaking,"

"He called again!" I shouted into the phone; my coworker was looking at me concerned everyone I work with knows what was going on.

"Are you with someone right now?" He asked, his voice was harder than usual, I think he was concerned.

"I'm at work," I said, looking around.

"Good, stay there, me and my partner will go to your place and check it out, it'd be best if you stayed with a friend until this is sorted out," He said firmly.

"Okay," I murmured. He hung up and I thought for a moment. I wanted to stay with someone I absolutely trusted but I was worried. What if this person hurt them? I didn't want to get my friends hurt. I settled on one of my best guy friends, he was always there for me, always had my back. I sent him a text asking if I could stay a few days with him. He agreed, I was slightly relieved, I wouldn't be sleeping alone, and I would finally feel like I won't be slaughtered in my sleep by whoever was stalking me. It felt like forever before my shift ended, the drive to his house was forever.

When you're in a scary or terrifying position, like not knowing if you're going to wake up the next day, or if the next time you wake up, there will be a knife to your throat, time slows. A second feels like a minute, a minute feels like an hour, an hour feels like a day, a day feels like a month. I don't listen to music when I drive anymore, I feel the need to constantly be alert. I feel the need to constantly be on the lookout. Trying to find a face for the voice. Did I want to know who the person behind the voice was? I finally pulled up to my friend's house. I walked up to the door and knocked, it quickly opened to see my friend looking down at me, he looked concerned.

"Hey, thanks for letting me stay with you for a couple nights," I thanked him a dozen times through text while I was working. I really couldn't tell him how much this meant to me. He led me inside making sure his doors and windows were locked. His living space was small so I slept on the small couch in the living room. I quickly fell asleep, I finally felt safe being somewhere other than my home and the bar. I woke up in the middle of the night to the sound of glass breaking but I quickly dozed back off.

I shot up when I heard a loud bang come from my friend's room. I heard his bed creaking and a gagging noise. I wanted to enter, but I was too scared. I felt my heart in my throat. I took a deep breath and made my way to the bedroom. Thankfully it was cracked. I peeked in and saw a man raise his knife and bring down my friends still body. I let out a quiet cry; but, it wasn't quiet enough to let me go unnoticed. The strange man whipped his head around and looked at me. I stumbled back and began to run down the hallway. Tripping over myself. I heard the man behind me. I grabbed my jacket and bag which were laying on the table, I made a beeline for the door but I wasn't quick enough. As soon as I pulled the door open a strong hand shut it easily and I felt a sharp piercing pain in my lower back; then another; then another. My legs collapsed, leaving me there laying in the doorway. My shirt felt wet. I noticed I was bleeding a lot, did this man stab me. Was I going to be his next victim?

Creatures in the Shadows

I was always scared of the dark. I see creatures in the shadows, they're vaguely humanoid. I laid in bed, my boyfriend lying next to me. I watched the shadows reach out at me. I looked down at the foot of the bed and I screamed, causing Kyle to shoot up. I grabbed the flashlight, and the thing dropped down; retreating back into the shadows. I crawled to the foot of my bed and looked under; nothing was there. I ran over to the light and turned it on before crawling back into bed.

"Are you okay?" Kyle asked, wrapping his arms around me. I didn't say anything. "Do you want to sleep with the light on to-night?" He asked. I nodded and laid back down and found myself drifting off to sleep. When I woke up, the room was filled with sunlight. I went out into the kitchen and Kyle was preparing me breakfast. The room is warm with the morning son.

"Morning," I groaned, rubbing my eyes.

"Morning, you sleep well?" He asked.

"No," I responded grumpily.

"You had me kind of shook last night," He responded, I could now tell that he was upset with me. "Have you considered talking to someone about this?" He murmured, "What if you get more violent?" He continued. I was taken aback, I didn't know how to respond.

"I won't," I managed.

"Can you promise that?" He questioned. I remained silent. "When should I make an appointment?" I asked.

"This morning, after breakfast," He said simply.

"I'm not hungry," I muttered.

"You always do this when you're upset, I just care about your wellbeing," He shot.

"What should I do?" I demanded. The room was filled with tension you could cut with a knife. I silently ate and we went about the day not talking to each other. I made a therapy appointment for the day after the next. The next morning the mood was better and we started talking again. After breakfast he did the dishes while I got dressed and ready to go. I knew deep down talking to a therapist might help. I was also scared, what if something more serious was wrong with me.

We climbed into his care and made our way to the office. He seemed rather pleased with himself. I watched the sun fall, and I felt my nerves grow uneasy. I eyed the darkness.

"Do you see that person?" Kyle asked. I saw a figure walking on the end of the road. It was far up, but you could see the outline sway back and forth like they were exhausted, or drunk.

"Yeah, I see them," I started leaning forward and squinting my eyes. They were too far to make out any detail about them.

"Should we pick them up?" Kyle asked.

"No," I murmured.

"Why not, they may need help?" He asked.

"What if it's someone who wants to jump us?" I shot. He sighed and nodded. The closer we got, the more and more I felt uneasy. Why couldn't I make out what they looked like by this point. I kept my eyes on the person. Kyle seemed to be uneasy too. "What's up?" I asked.

"Something seems off," He murmured.

"Do you want to pull off at the next exit and rest?" I asked. He shook his head.

"We're almost there, there wouldn't really be a point in stopping now only to stop again later," He said. I nodded. The person didn't seem to have an outline, it just looked like a person shaped shadow among the shadows. We finally passed the person up and I felt a bit more at ease and Kyle seemed to relax a bit. Another hour passed and he finally pulled off an exit and found a hotel for us. We went into a parking structure and we got out of the car.

"Are you okay?" He asked me to rub my back. I nodded and we made our way to the check in desk. When we got to our room I collapsed on the bed and sighed.

"That guy was so weird," I said, looking at the ceiling.

"It was, it was like he wasn't even there," Kyle said laying down next to me. He wrapped his arms around my waist and let out a sigh of content. When we woke up the next morning, we grabbed some of the free breakfast.

"Are you ready to meet the therapist?" He asked. I nodded. We made our way to the car. Why was it so dark in this structure; it seemed a lot lighter last night. There was a person standing by the car, I froze in my tracks. It looked like the shadows. Kyle stopped too. "What is that thing?" He asked, he stared wide eyed in terror at it.

"You see it too?" I asked. I didn't take my eyes off the twitching shadow being.

"Of course, I fucking see it!" He shouted. It turned around and began to stumble its way towards us.

Kyle grabbed my arm and started running. I spotted a fire door and pulled away from Kyle and made a beeline for the door. The thing stumbled towards me. As soon as it got close enough, I opened the door, flooding the place with light. I heard a high-pitched wail as the thing vaporized into nothing. I stayed in the door. I stayed in safety.

"I thought only you saw those things, what did you do?" He asked. He sounded angry.

"I didn't do anything!" I shouted back. I was scared, he saw that thing, that thing was real.

"Well you did something; those things were just in your head 2 days ago!" He shouted at me. I felt tears welling up in my eyes.

"I don't know what's happening, but I'm scared," I murmured. He nodded. I got my flashlight out and we walked to the car. I was shaking. I looked out the window, my heart rate refused to go down. I was on alert, looking for any other things. Kyle rubbed my knee, trying to comfort me.

We got to this large building, it was by a lake. He parked and sighed.

"Are you going to tell them that I saw it too?" He asked.

"I-I don't know," I murmured. He rubbed my back before getting out of the car. I climbed out and sighed. "I want to look at the water before we go in," I murmured. I walked over to the lake side and sat on the grass.

"Somehow, you made that thing real," Kyle said. His voice was dull and tired. We were both emotionally exhausted from today's experience.

"I don't know how, it's not possible, it's crazy," I murmured. I was thinking back to it. "It means that it really can kill me," I murmured.

"I won't let that happen," he promised. He sighed. "You know I love you right?" He asked. I gasped when he grabbed my throat. He began to squeeze. I couldn't breathe. I began to struggle against him. "You're dangerous," He repeated softly. I tried shaking my head. My head was spinning.

I reached up and drove my finger into his eye. He pulled back and covered his eyes.

"Can't you see you're a danger?" He shouted. I shook my head.

"I didn't do anything!" I shouted. He lunged at me and I pushed him back. He lost his footing and fell in the water. He popped up and I began to back up. He began to swim but stopped. A look of terror swept over his face.

"Something's under the water!" He shouted. His head fell under the water for a moment. "Help me!" He shouted. I shook my head. I saw the shadows reach up and pull him down. I ran to the edge of the water and strained my eyes to look into the water. I saw the shadows wrap themselves around him. I backed away. Staring in shock. Did I do this? Was this my fault? Am I really a danger?

Disowned

I looked around the restaurant. It was empty besides a small family eating over in a corner, enjoying their meal. I sighed and looked down at my phone. It was only 3 hours until the end of my shift, but it felt like it was years away. I began to play on my phone, it was about 20 minutes until I heard the bell notifying me that someone was coming inside. I put my phone in my back pocket and looked up and my heart sank all the way into a pit in my stomach. It was my grandma and my uncle. I wanted to get mad. I wanted to yell at them and tell them to get the hell out of the restaurant but that's just what they wanted me to do.

"Will there be two?" I asked. I'm lucky I just have to seat them. The waitress has to deal with them once I sit them down and give them their drinks. I led them to a table all the way in the back, out of sight from my podium.

"What will you two be having to drink today?" I asked. They both ordered black coffees. I went into the kitchen and poured them two cups of coffee and brought them back out, I wore a big fake plastic smile. There was no way I was going to let them have any satisfaction. "Your waitress will be right over to take your order." I said smiling. I went to turn away but my grandmother grabbed my wrist causing me to stop in my tracks.

"Your father misses you very much," She said.

"I don't care if he misses me," I muttered towards her before pulling my wrist from her and walking away. One of the waitresses walked over to me after a few moments.

"Are you okay?" She asked.

"Yeah, I'm fine, why do you ask?" I questioned, a bit surprised.

"You look like you're about to cry," she murmured, rubbing my arm.

"That old couple keeps asking about you, what should I tell them?" She asked. I shrugged.

"Nothing, just tell them you're not able to tell them personal information about the other employees." I stated. I was struggling to gather my composure. My anxiety levels were now through the roof. I don't know if I could handle this but I had to, I didn't really have a choice, and I wasn't going to let them bully me anymore.

"Why don't you talk to us anymore, like old times, remember?" My grandmother asked, I hadn't realized she had gotten up and walked over.

"Stop living in the past then," I muttered trying to keep my gaze forward.

"Just come over, for one dinner, that's all we ask, you can bring your daughter too," She offered. I sighed, I felt my tears welling up in my eyes.

"Just one dinner, then you'll leave me alone?" I asked, my voice was strained. My grandma nodded hesitantly. "When?" I asked, my tone was sharp and tense.

"Tomorrow night, after your shift," My grandma smiled. She reached out to tidy my hair and I pulled away sharply.

She looked angered by me pulling away but she didn't say any-thing. I was dreading it, but if it got them to leave me alone, then I was willing to go and have dinner with them. The next day I was dreading going to their house, work felt like it took the entire day. When I got off, I went home and grabbed my daughter and drove to my grandparents' house. I felt the pit of dread in my stomach. My mouth was watering, threatening to vomit my day's food. I held my daughter in one arm as I walked up the long path to the large, eerie house. When I rang the buzzer, the door opened before the bell could stop ringing out.

"Come in," My grandma urged. I stepped inside and kicked off my shoes easily. They led me to the dining room and I sat down at the table, my daughter in my lap.

"I didn't realize your daughter was so chubby," My grandma said with a slight chuckle. "Are you feeding her too much?" She asked.

"She's a baby, babies are supposed to be chubby," I stated firmly.

"Your mother was never that chubby as a baby, have you thought about putting her on a diet?" She asked.

"You know, do you ever consider that you're the reason your family doesn't talk to you?" I asked with a heat in my voice.

"That's not how you talk at a dinner table," My grandmother scolded. I scowled at her. "I think it'd be best for you to go wash your hands," she hissed. I stood up; my daughter still in my arms, there was no way I was going to leave her alone with this woman. I walked up the stairs to their second floor. There was a bathroom right and on the left. I noticed something walking past the doorway at the end of the hall. I shrugged it off as my deadbeat uncle. I went inside the bathroom, putting the toilet lid down and setting down my daughter on top of it. I scrubbed my hands violently. I jumped when the door creaked slightly open. When I checked the door there was no one there; I grabbed my daughter and went back downstairs. Something felt off.

"Is my uncle here?" I quizzed. My grandfather looked confused.

"What do you mean?" He asked.

"I just saw someone walk past the door upstairs, I thought it could be my uncle," I responded.

"No, he hasn't lived here for three months," My grandmother said, shaking her head. "Must be the shadows playing tricks on your head," She added with a chuckle; she made uncomfortable eye contact with my grandfather.

"It wasn't just dancing shadows, it was a person walking past a doorway, are you not concerned?" I asked. "You're at least not going to check?" I asked.

"No, who would want to break in here, we have to drag our own family here," My grandmother said sweetly. I felt uneasy, why are they so okay with someone possibly being here. My grandmother set a plate piled with food in front of me.

I pushed the food around with my fork before taking the smallest of bites. There was a loud thump coming from upstairs.

"What was that?" I demanded.

"It was nothing, just the pipes," My grandmother responded with a smile. I stood up.

"I don't feel comfortable with having my baby here," I stated.

"Don't leave yet," My grandmother said, standing up quickly. Her voice was sharp and shrill.

"Well there are strange noises, things moving around upstairs, I just don't feel safe," I shot, quickly gathering up my things.

"It's nothing, it's an old house," My grandfather said simply.

"I'm not going to risk putting my baby in danger," I stated. I picked up my baby and began walking towards the door. When I left, I turned around one last time and saw a light on in one of the upstairs windows. My heart was beating in my throat. I saw something big walk in front of the window, it was too big to be a person. I watched my grandparents clean up, they looked angry.

Their eyebrows furrowed in absolute rage, they were shouting at each other. I saw something walk past the entrance to the dining room. I turned around and began to walk quickly towards my car. I strapped my baby into her car seat tightly, making sure the seatbelt was secured. I got into the driver's side and shakily put on my own seat belt. I looked into their dining room one last time. I gasped when I saw my grandmother suspended in the air.

My grandfather was banging on the passenger window of my car, my baby started wailing, upset and the sudden yelling and banging. I glanced back at my grandmother and she was still floating, though she was covered in blood, I couldn't make out what was happening to her. I looked back at my grandfather; he was pleading through the window. I twisted my key starting the car, I threw the car in reverse and looked at my grandfather, my face fixed in a sad scowl. I pressed the gas lurching backwards into the street. My grandfather took two steps to try and chase us. Something stopped him, like something grabbing his shoulder, his shirt tore and created as he bagged to bleed. He was lifted into the air. I stared up at him, my heart racing in my chest, my daughter still wailing in the back seat.

He, like my grandmother, was pulled into the air, he was screaming even louder. I spun my wheels and put my car in Drive and started down the street, watching my grandfather through the rearview mirror. I tried staying under the speed limit, looking back at the road every few seconds. I saw blood rushing down his body and dripping onto the pavement. His body fell on the concrete. My heart jumped into my throat, I knew I was next; I screamed out as whatever the thing was rocked the car violently. My daughter is screaming even louder than before. I decided to drive even faster, narrowly missing hitting other cars. I regretted waiting to leave their house. I tried to act like I wasn't terrified getting my daughter ready for bed. She seemed to have forgotten the horror she witnessed earlier. I sat on the edge of her bed as she began to doze off.

When I heard her quiet snores, I rose up from her bed and went into my bathroom. I began to wash my face and go through the motions of going to bed myself, I tried to ignore what I saw earlier that night. I jumped when something walked past the door. I felt my knees knock together, as if they were about to give out. I turned around and leaned against the counter. Trying to keep myself from falling down. I held my breath and strained my ears. I wanted to throw up, my stomach knotted in fear. I shakily took a step forward and my leg refused to stand. I had to rest my hand on my knee to keep it from buckling. I was trying to catch my breath, but it felt as if all the air in the room was sucked out. I rested my hand on the door handle and opened it all the way. I peered down the hallway, nothing. I let out a sigh of relief. I went to my room, it was nice to regain strength in my leg, but my heart was still racing. I turned my light on and flopped down on my bed. I pulled the covers over me; I didn't want to sleep in the dark tonight.

I awoke in the middle of the night with a loud crash in the living room. It sounded as if something pushed a bookshelf over. I grabbed my phone and saw the battery was dead, I plugged my phone in and the blinking 0% mocked me. I stood up and walked to the door and opened it. I looked up the hallway and my daughter's door, it was how I left it. I walked down the hall; my legs shook violently. I drug my hand against the wall trying to comfort myself. I screamed when I turned the corner, a large shadow stood in the center of the room. I felt my knees give out and I found myself scrambling backwards. My back hit the wall and I stared at it in fear, waiting for it to do to me what it did to my family, but it never happened. My eyes darted to my child's room when she started crying, but when I looked back, the thing was gone.

Winter Warning

My family was piled in our car. We were going to this lodge up north, I wasn't paying attention to the planning much, I hated family vacations. I always preferred to spend the time at home while they did their own thing on vacation. Since it's Christmas though, I was forced to come along. When we got to the lodge it was beautiful; it looked old. Something felt off about it; it screamed something wrong. I climbed out of the car along with my parents.

"What do you think?" My dad asked.

"It's breathtaking," I said, trying to hide my discomfort with the place.

"It really is something else," Mom added. We grabbed our bags and headed inside; the atmosphere felt even more distorted inside. I felt like I was being watched. I looked over to my mom and she looked just as uncomfortable as me.

We checked in and we got our room keys. We hurried to our rooms, my dad wanted to relax, but I knew there was no way I would be able to relax. As soon as I got in my room, I put my bag by the table and plopped down on the bed. I stared at the tv and turned it on before laying back. I jumped when I saw something move out of the corner of my eye, but I really didn't think anything of it. I just assumed it was the shadows dancing as I began to doze off. I pulled the covers over myself. The blankets were thick and scratchy. Despite the discomfort I found myself slowly drifting off into a deep sleep. I shot up when there was loud knocking at the door. I felt my heart racing as I approached the door, when I opened it my dad was standing there frustrated.

"We were texting you," He stated.

"I fell asleep, sorry," I muttered.

"Why didn't you sleep in the car on the way here?" He asked as I left my room and followed him through the halls.

"Because the backseat of the car with all our bags is cramped and uncomfortable," I responded.

"You can be grateful," My father responded.

"You asked me why I didn't sleep in the backseat, I told you why I physically couldn't sleep," I huffed while walking down the hall.

I sighed, there was no use arguing with him. He grabbed my arm and drug me to the restaurant built into the hotel, I sighed as I slipped into the booth next to my mom.

"What's wrong?" She asked.

"Nothing," I muttered. I looked around the dining room and I noticed mannequins. It made me feel slightly uneasy. Why were there just random mannequins? They were all wearing quite festive Christmas sweaters. We ate dinner in a tense silence, it was almost suffocating.

"What?" He barked at me.

"I didn't say anything, nothing's wrong," I defended myself.

"Well then why are you always getting an attitude?" He asked.

"I don't have an attitude," I responded, trying not to raise my voice.

I was aware of the eyes of the people around me, watching my father begin to sit up from anger. My eyes flicked from the people to the mannequins; it was almost as if they were looking too, watching this action unfold. It made me feel uneasy. My father noticed the eyes on him as well and he returned to eating, his fork slammed into the plate with loud clunks.

After dinner was over, we returned to our hotel rooms. I watched reruns of older TV shows when I got a text from my mother asking me if I wanted to explore. I eagerly got out of bed and met her outside her hotel room. We made our way to the elevator as we made small talk, as soon as the door closed.

"What floor do you want to go to?" She asked. I pressed the button for the basement. There was a long silence, nothing but the cheery elevator music until the elevator shook to a stop at the bottom most level. Leaving the elevator and turning on my phone's flashlight I shined it against the moist concrete floor. The room smelled damp and musty. My mother and I made small conversation as we roamed about. Our footsteps echoed off the walls.

I rounded a corner and froze. My mom walked right into me, knocking me off balance, the entire room was filled with mannequins.

"Jesus Christ," I murmured under my breath. Their heads were all facing us; almost as if we caught them in the act of doing something they shouldn't be. There was a strong smell, almost like rotting meat. "I think we should leave," I said breathlessly.

"Why?" My mom questioned.

"Something doesn't feel right," I responde. My voice was tight, and I could barely force out the whisper.

"Are you scared?" She teased. I nodded, I could no longer let out any words, I felt like if I opened my mouth I would just vomit. She sighed and hesitantly led the way back to the elevator. My legs felt like Jell-O. When we got to the elevator, I let out a sigh of relief.

"Are you okay?" My mom asked, she was genuinely concerned. I nodded.

"I think so," I whispered. When we got to our floor I rushed into my room and locked the door before throwing myself onto the bed and pulling the covers over my head. I knew I wasn't going to get any sleep that night. I laid there, watching the shadows dance over the covers, flinching whenever I saw something that looked vaguely human like. When morning came, I was relieved. I tossed my blankets off and quickly got changed and headed down to breakfast. I saw my mom sitting there, drinking coffee. I went to the pastry box and grabbed a couple cherry cheese danishes and sat down with her.

"I'm surprised dad isn't with you," I said with a big smile

"He was gone when I woke up, I assume he went to get gas or to get soda," She said with a simple shrug.

"Any Plans for the day?" I asked.

"No, why? Did you want to do something?" She asked.

"I just was curious, I'll see you later," I chuckled. I got up and went to the elevator. I don't know why but I felt the burning need to go to the basement again. I pressed the button and the elevator groaned to a start, it creaked all the way down and shook before the elevator doors slid open. Already I felt the fear settling in the pit of my stomach, I regretted eating such a sugary breakfast. I took one step after another, my knees shook violently. I turned the corner and saw all the mannequins; they were all in different positions than what they were left in. I made my way over, hoping to see if anything would have caused them to move. The closer I got I saw that there was blood on the floor. There was a door behind the mannequins and there was a light on underneath it.

"Is anyone there?" I called out to the door.

"Sweetie is that you?" I heard my dad call from the other side of the door. My stomach tightened, my father's voice was off, it was like it was being played through an old speaker. I moved between the mannequins, growing closer and I felt like the buzzing of the lights above grew louder. I grasped the door handle and glanced behind me. They were all looking at me. I pulled the door open and what I saw made me sick. I saw my dad's skin forced over a mannequin.

"What's wrong, you look sick," My dad's voice came from the mannequin. It stepped forward and I stumbled backwards landing on my butt. I scrambled to my feet and turned to run; the mannequins were blocking my way out. I shoved my way through them, they fell and broke apart like Styrofoam. A strong hand grabbed my shoulder and I struggled out of the grasp and ran to the elevator.

I frantically pressed the button to my floor and ran to my parents' room and began to pound on the door. My mom opened it and looked at me confused. I rushed inside and grabbed the car keys.

"We have to go," I said firmly, my voice was shaking, worse, I was shaking.

"What?" She asked, confused.

"Get your things, we're leaving," I said. She packed her bag and we left. I never told her what I saw.

The Greyman

I just moved into the apartment I grew up in, I am surprised it was still operational let alone vacant. It was under new management though. I set my boxes in my parents' old room. I looked at the dusty white paint. It's been almost fifteen years since I've last seen this place, but all of a sudden I felt like the second grader I was when I first moved in so many years ago. It felt like nothing changed, the fresh spring breeze outside, the slight creak of the floor. I felt like a kid again, everything looked the same for the most part, a bit worse for wear. I unloaded my boxes, eager to make the place feel like my own. I had made a point of going until the sun was completely down. I wasn't done by nightfall, but I made a lot of progress.

I moved to unpacking the boxes and hanging up some of the pictures I had. It didn't take long to feel exhaustion weighing on my body, I began to feel fatigued from everything. I decided to get ready for bed and laid out my sleeping bag. When I finally laid down I couldn't manage to fall asleep, the silence was unsettling and eerie. It felt like I laid there for hours before I found myself quietly getting out of my sleeping bag. I stepped outside onto the patio. I remember standing out here during a storm, and watching the rain run down the glass. I look out and noticed something in the long section of trees that was a few yards away. I squinted and I thought I saw a long gray creature crouched behind a bush. Its arms and legs were inhumanly long. Its face looked loose against its skull, almost hanging off.

I jumped when I heard the door open down the hall, I watched my neighbor lock the door behind her, she was dressed up. We shared a brief smile before heading down the stairs. I looked back to where I saw the creature that had disappeared. I watched my neighbor walk down the sidewalk, keys in hand. I searched the greenery and I saw nothing like what that creature looked like. I went back inside, making sure to lock my door and close my blinds before laying back down. It didn't take me long to finally drift off into a deep dreamless sleep.

I woke up late the next morning. My muscles ached and I felt like I hadn't even slept. I got up and went to the kitchen to make myself a cup of coffee and breakfast. I sat on the counter, surrounded by boxes and furniture. The day felt like it was a year, I was sorer than I was that morning, but thankfully all the furniture was inside. Tomorrow I could return the moving van. Again, that night I had a hard time sleeping, it could be the aching muscles, or being in a not new, new place. Once again, I went on the patio, hoping to clear my head. For minutes everything was still, not even wind shook the branches of the trees. Suddenly some bushes and branches started violently shaking; I squinted my eyes, trying to see what moved. Deep down I knew what it was; I wanted to find evidence it wasn't what I thought it was.

I saw something slowly crawl out of the wooded area. It looked insect-like, it was a pale gray tone, like a corpse, it had long arms and legs that bent outwards. My eyes met with it, and I felt my heart sink, my mouth fell open, but the only thing that came out was a near silent squeak. The thing suddenly moved at lightning speed towards the first-floor door that led to the second-floor apartments; the silence cut by the door shaking against the door frame, it sounded like it was throwing itself against the door. I felt my heart racing in my chest, I was frozen in fear. Soon the thing stopped, there was an eerie silence. After what felt like hours, I managed to step backwards. I locked the door behind me when I got inside, making sure the sliding door was locked as well. I climbed back into the sleeping back on the floor and stared at the dim ceiling. My heart was racing, my mind spinning. I couldn't help but watch the window, waiting for the slightest movement. There was no way I was sleeping.

The next morning I had shakily made myself breakfast, I was searching for what that creature could possibly be, hoping that it was a dog or something of the like. After I had finished breakfast I took the Uhaul back, it was nice getting out of the apartment, feeling free of the weight of worry. I dreaded going home, but I needed to get the furniture in place. I listened to music and podcasts, hoping to fight away the thoughts of the creature. Everything felt as if it weighed a ton, but by the end of the day most of the furniture was in place. I flopped down on the couch, exhausted. I watched the trees dance in the wind and my eyes began to grow heavy. I couldn't stop the pull of sleep.

I had awoken to darkness, the sun had gone down and I had no idea what time it was or how long I was asleep. I quickly turned on the light, I felt skittish and uneasy. I sat down on the floor and eyed the window, waiting for movement. I watched the shadows of the tree sway and bob in the wind, but nothing like the thing I saw during the prior nights. The bobbing of the trees made my drowsiness worse and I laid down. I jolted awake at the sound of glass breaking in the guest room. I strained my ears to listen but I just couldn't hear anything. I shakily got to my feet and walked down the hallway, the floor creaking so familiarly under my feet.

When I got to the guest room I hesitated opening the door. I felt my blood pulsing in my fingertips and heard my heart beating in my ears. I held my breath and slowly turned the handle. I prepared to run if that thing was in my room. I swung the door open and the first thing I saw was bloody glass on the floor of my bedroom. On my bed lay a dead cat. I ran out of the room having felt my stomach summersalt. After I had finished throwing up I shakily called the police, trying to figure out what I would say. There was no way I could be honest about what happened, I would be sent to a looney bin.

The day flew by, I wanted to leave, but I had to stay and talk to the officers. Once they were done asking questions they left me alone to deal with the dead cat. I didn't want to go near it but they didn't get paid to deal with it. I wrapped it up in the sheets and eased my way outside, it took everything in me to not throw up. I finally let out a sigh of relief when I threw it out. I ordered a steam cleaner and went to sit in the living room. I felt like I was going crazy. The next morning, I found myself looking for apartments in the city, I didn't want to stay here after this investigation was over. When it got late I decided to go to bed in my room, maybe sleeping in the living room is making me struggle with sleeping.

I awoke to sounds in the living room. I creeped over to the door and cracked the door and tried to see down the dark hallway. I couldn't see anything through the darkness. I couldn't stop myself from imagining something just past the darkness. The lightswitch was on the other end of the hallway. I shut my door and grabbed my phone before going back to the door and shining the light down the hallway, the living room was empty from what I saw. A few days came and went, the police showing up every so often. I decided to finally get out and I went for a walk. I found myself walking down the old bike path. I made it to the end of the bike path and I turned around and started the walk back. The sun was setting so I decided to go to the park next to the apartment. They did a lot of work on the park, what was once just 3 slides and a set of monkey bars, was replaced by a proper playscape.

I remember when I was a child playing on it all day with my friends from the complex. I sighed. I noticed something moving. I turned around and saw the familiar grayish tint of flesh in some nearby bushes. I immediately got up and began to walk home, it was less than a 5- minute walk, especially if I'm walking at a brisk pace. I shook as I heard something behind me, it sounded as if bones were cracking and popping, there was an unsettling slapping sound against the pavement behind me. I wanted to look behind me but I knew there was no way that would go well. I tried to avoid speeding up in fear of it pouncing on me. I finally made it to my apartment building. I opened the door and slammed it shut behind me before running up the stairs to my apartment.

I peered out from the porch and I saw it investigating the door, the thing was literally right behind me. I had no idea what this thing wanted, or if it wanted to terrorize or hurt me. It looked up at me, it had sockets where the eyes would be. I gasped as I saw it climb onto the wall like a spider. I backed away from the window and pressed myself against my door, blindly fumbling for the handle. I froze when it climbed into the view. It slammed one of its long misshapen hands against the glass making me jump and let out a small yelp. It did it again and again, in a slow, tediously rhythmic fashion. Our eyes remained locked, as if in a staring contest, my eyes burned and I felt my eyelids begin to twitch, demanding I shut my eyes for a brief moment. When I opened them again, it was gone, like it was never there. I took a deep breath and went back into the apartment. I went to the kitchen and got myself a glass of water and sipped from it slowly, trying to calm my nerves.

That night I was uneasy about going to sleep, but soon I couldn't stop myself from fading out into a blissful sleep. I woke up in the middle of the night to a loud squeak, like plastic rubbing against metal. I noticed the sliding glass door to the porch was ajar. I went over and shut it, clicking the lock closed and turned around, I saw the thing perched on the table, staring at me. I backed myself against the window, it slowly eased its way off the table, approaching me.

Never go to the Caves

It took about 6 hours to drive to the farm, but when we got out of the car it was all worth it. The air had a faint scent of smoke, the air was easy to breathe, it was refreshing and cool. The tall grass rustled in the wind. Nick popped the trunk and I grabbed my bag and the tent out of the tent. Rodney grabbed the cooler and Alicia grabbed both her bag and his. Nick locked the door and shut it and grabbed what was left in the trunk before slamming it shut and we bag the hike up to the farm house. We were going to set up behind the house. I helped Rodney put up the tent, while Nick went back to get the grill.

"Something feels off about this," Alicia said, looking around. "I think something is watching us," she added.

"What do you mean?" I asked.

"I don't know, I just feel uneasy," She responded.

"Is there anything that would make you feel safer, Rodney and I are here, Nick is on his way back probably with the grill," I quizzed.

"I don't know, it's probably stupid," She murmured.

"Well, if you don't feel better, just let me know," I said.

"I got it!" Rodney shouted, making both Alicia and I jump.

"Good job," I chuckled looking over my shoulder. I spotted Nick rounding the corner of the house with the grill. He looked over the trip already having to haul that up from the car.

"Right on time, we just finished the tent!" I Shouted with a grin on my face.

"I finished the tent," Rodney shot. Alicia and I giggled. Nick set the grill down and began to pour coal into it. I looked up at the clouds and watched them drift across the sky. I flinched when someone placed a paper plate in my lap.

"Thanks," I chuckled as I dug into the burger. By the time we all finished eating the sun was setting. "Want to go and explore?" I asked dumping my paper plate into a plastic bag tied to the cooler.

"It's almost dark," Alicia said curtly.

"I know, that's the point," I stated.

"I don't know, we're all tired, let's do it tomorrow night," Nick said stretching.

"Come on!" I excitedly pleaded.

"I really don't want to tonight," Alicia insisted. I sighed feeling a bit put out.

"Alright," I said softly. I climbed into the tent and rolled out my sleeping bag by the Velcro mesh window. Rodney and Alicia followed me inside while Nick stayed outside to clean up a bit more. After about five minutes he climbed into the tent and rolled out his own sleeping bag. I fell asleep rather quickly, but awoke hours later. I could hear the grass rustling in the wind, hearing the house creaking as it settled. I shot up when I thought I heard a twig snap. I began to breathe heavily, my eyes glued to the Velcro holding the piece of fabric covering the window in place. I shakily reached out and worked it open, trying to not make a sound. I tried to lift it and discreetly look out to see what it was. I saw something in the distance; it was gray and on all fours.

I let the flap fall, I didn't know how to feel, it's a farm and it wouldn't be surprising if a wild animal found its way onto the property. I laid down and tried to fall back asleep, I wanted to keep track of the animal outside. I guess I eventually fell asleep because I was startled awake by Nick climbing out of the tent. I stretched and a few bones in my back popped. I got up and went outside, the grill was already going with Rodney poking the coals.

"How'd you sleep?" He asked with a smile. I plopped down in my chair and pulled my feet off the ground. It was chilly outside.

"I saw an animal outside in the middle of the night," I yawned.

"What do you mean?" Nick asked, he perked up a bit. I pointed in the distance.

"Over there, I heard a twig snap and I looked outside. It was probably a gray fox or something," I started with a shrug. "Have you guys started coffee yet?"

"No, I just woke up about half an hour ago, the fire just now started roaring," Rodney said grumpily.

"Get it going, I need to wake up," I said eagerly.

"Do you want to wake Alicia up, or should I?" Nick asked.

"You can," I said, "You can also grab a sweater out of my bag, it's cold as hell," I asked. He nodded and headed into the tent. "How'd you sleep?" I asked Rodney.

"I slept like a rock," He responded dully. He set a kettle on the grill.

"Hey guys," Alicia said groggily as she climbed out of the tent, Nick threw my sweater at me and I caught it almost falling back.

"Why isn't the coffee done?" Alicia asked, sitting in her chair which was next to mine.

"He just put the kettle on," I stated. She could only really muster a groggy yawn and leaned back like she was trying to fall back asleep.

"After we have our coffee and breakfast, we should explore the house," I stated excitedly. "It's daylight out so we don't have to worry about being too spooked by whatever is in that house," I said excitedly. Everyone agreed with varying levels of excitement. We took turns getting dressed as Rodney made coffee and putting them in our travel mugs. I led the march around the house. We stepped over the tall grass, and tripped on knotted grass. Soon I was climbing up onto the porch, the wood creaking under my feet. I turned around to see the others jogging up onto the porch, the same grin plastered to their faces as the one I had plastered on mine.

"So, do you want to start from the ground floor and move up?" I asked.

"That doesn't sound too bad," Alicia said with a huge grin. I grabbed the handle and pulled the huge, heavy door open. It creaked loudly as it drifted open. A cold wind rushed out, and we got hit with the strong scent of burnt wood. I stepped inward and the floor let out a long creak.

"Whoa," I chuckled looking around. It looked as if it wasn't even cleaned out, old burnt furniture sat in the same places they were as the first night of the fire. I walked over to the couch and placed my hand, the fabric crumbled under my touch. I wiped my hand off on my jeans and walked over to the bookcase. I pushed books around and most of them turned to ash and crumbled. I grabbed a metal decoration and picked it up, it looked partially melted. I tossed it on the ground. Alicia jumped. Shortly after the decoration thumped on the floor, there was a loud thump from the basement.

"What was that?" I asked. I eyed the door to the basement.

"I don't know," Nick said, reaching into his waistband and pulling out a gun.

"What are you doing?" I asked.

"Being safe," He whispered to me. We all stood in silence, the faint creaking of the house in the wind. There was another echo-ey thump in the basement.

"Alright, that's not coincidental," Alicia whispered. I moved towards the basement door with nick right behind me. My hand shook as I reached out for the handle. I grabbed it and yanked it open; revealing a long stairwell. I could hear my heart beating in my ears; it felt like my heart was in my throat. There was a long silence as we all stared down the stairway, my knees shook violently.

"Who's going down?" Alicia asked.

"I will," Nick said, starting down the stairs, I could see the fear in his eyes, I felt bad for him. I started down the stairs behind him. I jumped when the stairs behind me creaked. Rodney was stepping down the stairs and Alicia was shortly behind him. I felt a bit more comfortable with them backing us up. When we got to the bottom of the steps it didn't look like your typical basement, it looked like a mouth of a cave.

"Let's turn around," Alicia insisted.

"If there's a cave, it could have just been some rocks," Nick said simply.

"But why is there a cave down here?" Alicia questioned. We continued to ease forward silently. "I'm sorry I can't stay," Alicia said, running back up the stairs. Nick continued inward into the cave, trying to see how deep it went.

"Did you know anything about this?" Nick asked. I shook my head.

"Why would I know?" I asked. He didn't respond, there was a loud wet slapping coming from the inside of the cave. Nick jumped at the rapid and loud sound and ran up the stairs, abandoning Rodney and I alone with whatever was in the cave. I began to stumble backwards, tripping over a rock and falling on my ass. I saw something moving in the shadows of the cave, coming closer, the light coming from the door, barely illuminating the cave mouth. I saw a gray human-like creature. It looked bloated and hair hung off it in whisps. Its nose was long and its teeth were sharp and its eyes large, black and bug-like. I got to my feet and started up the stairs and the thing began to trip up the stairs. Rodney followed me up, his hand reached out to grab the railing but missed his foot slipped and he stumbled down a few steps, the thing grabbing his ankle and began to drag him down the steps and into the cave.

I continued running up the stairs and out of the house. I rounded the corner and saw Alicia with her bag and my bag, and Nick with Rodney's bag. I shook my head as I followed them up the path to the car, I looked behind me and saw a four-legged creature, catching up. I threw myself into the car and shut and locked my door. Alicia was struggling with her back-door handle. Nick climbed in slamming and locking his own door. Alicia finally ripped the door open falling in face first before sitting up and locking the door.

"Where's Rodney?" She asked, she looked like she was going to cry, I couldn't really blame her.

"That thing got him," I panted out. My chest heaved violently as I struggled to catch my breath. With a loud thump the thing was on the hood of the car, it looked like a naked old woman. Its hair was matted and tangled. The hands and forearms were covered in blood, it made me sick thinking about the possibility that it was Rodney's blood. "What the fuck!" Nick shouted. He put the car in reverse and slammed on the gas. The thing fell off the hood before looking around and scurrying back towards the house.

Puddle of the Dead

I sat on a bench outside of a cabin, trees swayed peacefully in the wind, it was a beautiful day. The clouds covered the sun, leaving it chilly and shady. I stood up and stretched, my back popping. I went back into my cabin and grabbed a bottle of water and my camera. I could really go for a quick hike. I hung my camera from my neck and walked out locking my cabin and heading into the woods. I loved the smell. The ground was moist, like it was raining all night. A large gust of wind made the leaves rattle against each other in the wind. I continued to trudge up the path, there were moments where I struggled to keep my footing. felt a droplet of water hit my face, and I looked up. The clouds twisted and danced above my head, I brushed it off as the trees.

I continued to trudge forward, pausing to snap shots here and there. I got to the top of a large hill and looked down and saw an abandoned building, I looked behind myself and I lost sight of the camp, no cabins, no fires, no smoke, nothing. How long have I been walking? I continued forward, excited to be able to explore an abandoned building. I jogged down the hill, easily picking up speed. I slowed down as I hit the bottom of the tall hill. I walked over to the building, it looked as if it was about to collapse. It was surrounded by a rotting wood fence. I began to walk over to the building, the grass was tall and overgrown, a strong breeze made the grass whisper and shake. I began to walk around the building, the ground was wet and my feet sunk into the mud slightly.

I wonder why the ground was still so wet, it hadn't rained in weeks. I continued to trudge around the building, looking for a way in, it would be a great photo opportunity. The mud squelched under my feet as I walked, trying to hold me in place. Soon I got to the side of the building and saw a broken window. I quickly made my way over and peered inside. The inside smelled musty and like rotting wood. I used my camera bag to break the remnants of the glass in so I could safely climb inside. My feet landed on the carpet with a squish as water puddled in the indents of my feet. I looked up and saw about a dozen leak marks on what was left of ceiling panels. Wires hung loosely from the ceiling, lights were cracked or missing. The room looked like an abandoned classroom; the only thing left was a scratched chalkboard. I walked across the room and tried to open the door, but it wouldn't budge. The wood had swollen and warped to the point it was wedged firmly within the metal frame. I sighed and walked back to the window, climbing out with ease.

I continued to walk around the building looking for another entrance. I rounded the corner and tripped. Landing hands and knees into a deep puddle up to my elbows. I quickly tried to stand up but I was stuck, the mud had a hold on my hands. I began to lean back trying to free at least one hand when I looked up, there were two skeletal bodies in the mud. Skin and tissue hung loosely from their skulls as if they had been here for a while. I screamed and tried to pry myself free. I felt the mud begin to loosen on my right hand as I yanked it to freedom, before trying to pull my left hand out. I kept looking at the skeletons before noticing how small they are. They were children when they died. I stumbled backwards as my hand lurched free. I quickly steadied myself before trying to free my knees. My breath was getting quick and I panicked. One of my knees lurched free and I quickly freed my second leg. Running as fast as I could back towards the hill, the mud and water weighing my clothes down.

Once I hit the bottom of the hill, I collapsed to my knees and looked over my shoulder. Everything was absolutely still, not even a whisper from the wind to make the trees shiver. I found myself forcing myself to my feet, my legs aching from struggling to free myself from mud and continuing to run up the hill. I won't tell anyone about this, how would I tell anyone about this?

The Things in the Sewers

I had just punched out. I looked out the window and saw the street stories below, cars were speeding on the roads and people were on the street corners talking. I made my way to the elevator and pressed the button to go to the ground floor. I waited for a few moments, complete silence besides the soft beeping of the numbers above the elevator, letting me know how close it was to my floor. Soon the doors slid open and I stepped on as I continued to watch the night life of the world below. I noticed a car; it was one I knew well from my past. A man who I no longer wanted to see was waiting just past the downstairs doors; I knew he couldn't come in, but he knew I had to leave.

I pressed the button for the basement, I know I wasn't supposed to be down there, but there might be a janitorial exit or something that I could leave out of. The elevator stopped on the ground floor and the doors opened for a split second before I began to press the close button in a near panic. The doors loudly slammed shut and continued its journey to the basement. Once again, the elevator came to a halt and the doors slammed open. I was instantly hit with the smell of mildew and dust. I stepped off the elevator onto the cool damp concrete. I stepped forward a few more steps and saw a hallway to my left, dimly lit by a red emergency light. I followed it hoping to find an exit around the side of the building, but it led me to a large spacious room and yet another hallway.

The room was home to large machines that I didn't know the purpose of and down the hall there was bridge going over a muddy looking river, I assumed it was the sewer system. I knew I should turn around, everything in me said I shouldn't continue, but I knew I couldn't face that man either. My feet carried me down the hallway,

I heard my feet against the metal bridge, I looked up and down and saw an archway. I walked through the arch and the darkness engulfed me. There was something unsettling about the darkness, like there was something just out of sight, walking with me, timing each step perfectly with mine so I wouldn't hear it. I saw the end of the tunnel, a flickering light letting me know that I would be safe soon. I picked up my pace, my breath quickened.

When I came to the end of the tunnel, I saw something odd, a doll on the floor, laying there, it looked like it was long abandoned by a child. There was much on its porcelain face and hands. Thin cracks stretched across her face; her blank stare went right past me. I nudged her with my foot and there was an audible squelch and a strange liquid oozed out. I stepped back and looked around, I was in a small room, I looked where I came, you could barely make out the dim light at the end of the tunnel. I looked at the second archway, leading me deeper into the maze. I continued deeper, I couldn't explain why I decided to continue, could be morbid curiosity, but as I looked back I thought I saw the doll move ever so slightly.

This walkway was a lot shorter than the first one, I entered another tunnel with a murky brownish green color. I heard a giggle behind me and I whipped my head around, the doll no longer was laying on the floor, I couldn't see the rest of the room. I was tempted to just head back to the surface, pretend that I never ventured down here. I heard the patter of tiny footsteps behind me. I spun back around and something disappeared behind a wall to another archway. Everything in me screamed to run, but I didn't. I forced my feet forward, one step after another, curiosity overtook me. Another tunnel, this one was longer than the first one. I stared down at it, I couldn't even see the end, was there even an end? One foot moved forward, then the second. I couldn't stop myself.

I walked for what felt like ten minutes, I still saw no light at the end of the tunnel and there was no longer light behind me. I stopped and sighed. I couldn't see anything. I couldn't even see the wall, there was nothing. I turned around and that's when I heard it. A gentle pattering on the floor made me whip my head around.

"Hello?" I called out. Hoping to hear a voice, someone could help me find my way out. I waited a few moments. "Hello?" I called out once again. My hope was fleeting as quickly as it swelled in my chest. I continued to walk the way I came, hoping that any minute, I'll see the light, and I could get out of here and go home. I walked for 5 minutes, it felt, and still nothing. I began to count to 60 in my head. Once I hit six minutes, the panic set in. Was I walking longer than I thought I was? I began to run, my head spinning, a primal fear sunk in my stomach, making me want to vomit.

My pace picked up, my footsteps echoing in my ears. A soft giggle made me grind to a halt. My momentum almost threw me on the floor.

"I heard you!" I shouted out. I spun around. "Please, I need help!" I pleaded. Another giggle made me turn once more, straining my eyes to see something, anything. I don't know why, but I started running in one direction, the sound of tiny steps was right on my heels. I wanted to look behind me, I wanted to see what was chasing me, but I knew if I slowed my pace, even for a second, I was going to die. I pushed myself harder than before, I was wheezing, gasping for breath. I soon saw it. The dim light, no smaller than the head of a needle. I was scared. Everything in my body ached, and I couldn't shake the sound of the steps behind me. The sounded so small and delicate, but it's moving at impossible speeds.

The light began to grow rapidly. I sprinted out the tunnel and into the next, not daring to rest. The steps behind me wouldn't be dull or slow. There was no panting, no exhaustion. A childish giggle rang out, another rush of adrenaline pushed me to run faster. My feet stung as they smacked against the concrete. I made it into the last room and ran through the tunnel. I was almost there. I quickly saw the basement door separating the system to the building. As I rushed through the arch of safety; I grabbed the door and slammed it shut, in the process to look behind me. I only got a split second before the door shook the frame. The image of a doll standing there burned into my mind, but that wouldn't be possible, couldn't be possible.

When I approached my building, I saw 2 cop cars and some vans and a man climbing up with a bag slung over his shoulder.

"What's going on?" I asked one of the cops. He readily ignored me. I sighed and watched and tried to follow the man with the bag. Curiosity consumed me. He approached another group of men and opened the bag and they all looked inside.

I stood on my tip toes trying to see what they were hiding in there. I thought I could see tiny plastic shoes. I approached the group and the man quickly shut the bag and hid it behind him like he was a child trying to hide something.

"What's going on?" I demanded once more.

"Um, apparently there was something hidden in the sewer and we're trying to find out what," The man replied simply.

"Do you know what might be hidden down there, I see you have a bag," I said, trying to peer behind the man's back.

"We can't disclose that until the police make an official report," The man responded awkwardly.

"Come on, I live right there, please?" I begged. The men shared a look.

"I ask because I was down there earlier, and I saw something weird," I said honestly. The men nodded at each other. The man opened the bag for me and I almost fell backwards when I saw what was inside. It was the doll.

Holes in the Floor

I stood up from our couch and began to make my way to the kitchen. I felt my foot hit wood, then wood break, my ankle catching on the sharp edge. I yelled out and yanked my foot out and fell back onto the couch. I looked at my ankle and there was a half inch cut bleeding profusely. I sighed and began to limp to the bathroom to tend to my wound. I heard the sound of wood and quickly shifted my weight onto my hurt foot to avoid catching my other foot as the wood fell out from under it. I yelled out as my knee buckled as a sharp pain shot through my leg. I managed to rush the rest of the way to the bathroom. I sat on the toilet lid and began to press toilet paper to the wound to try and slow down the blood. I pulled the damp toilet paper from my ankle and got alcohol out of the drawer and dumped it on my ankle violently, tensing for the pain.

"Fuck me!" I shouted, leaned back and clenched my teeth. I grabbed bandages and began to tightly bind my ankle. I heard the front door open and close. "Be careful!" I shouted from the bathroom.

"What happened?" My mother asked.

"I don't know," I responded. I heard the creaking of my mom moving across the living room to the bathroom. She appeared in the doorway. I made my way back to the living room. "That's certainly unfortunate, " I said, peering into the hole expecting to see the downstairs neighbor's apartment. I was shocked to see a dingy looking basement, I saw pipes and wires. "Look at that," I said, looking down. She peered down, but didn't look as puzzled as I felt.

"It must be between the apartments, the pipes could be building up moisture and it naturally weakened the wood," she said with a comforting smile.

"I'm going to cover these up with some wood or something, you should call maintenance," I said, grabbing my keys and pulling on my sneakers. I ran down the three flights of stairs to the basement and looked around. There were a few locked doors I couldn't look behind but I didn't see any possible way we could see what we saw in our apartment.

I sighed and went into the back portion of the building, I found 2 slabs of wood and brought them upstairs and laid them on top of the holes and sat on the couch. I still felt uneasy about the holes, something about it didn't seem right. A few days passed and the maintenance man has yet to show up to fix the hole. My curiosity began to eat away at me. I lifted up a slab of wood and peered into the hole. It was dimly lit to close to no light getting in. I jerked back when I thought I saw something move all the way at the bottom. My stomach did a flip and I stared at the wood not blinking.

I don't know how long I sat frozen before I crawled slowly back to the hole and lifted the board once again. I strained my eyes and focused, what I saw had to be a trick of the light, nothing can be down there. I stared intensely into the hole and I saw two pale twig light arms reach out and grasp the sides of the walls leading up, as if it was getting ready to pull itself up, pull itself closer to me. I stood up and ran out of the apartment and sat on the carpet separating my neighbor's door from mine. So many things are rushing around my head. I strained my ears to hear if the thing left the hole. I hesitantly brought my head to the floor, peering into the apartment. I laid there for maybe 10 minutes before an arm reached out, knocking the slab off the hole and reaching out, grabbing blindly for something, grabbing blindly for me.

"Holy shit," I whispered. The arm eventually receded down the hole. I stood up, shaking violently. I made my way to my feet and re-entered the apartment, I was currently questioning how good of an idea it was but I wasn't really thinking about that. I sat on the couch, pulling my feet up off the floor and turned on the tv, I stared at the 2 boards on the floor. I jumped violently when the door opened and my friend walked in. "What's wrong with you? She asked, laughing. Her eyes went to the holes in the floor. "Oh shit, what happened?" She asked.

"I don't know, I saw something down there though, look down there, slowly, and quietly," I murmured, my voice was a near whisper, my throat was tight and pained.

"What are you talking about, are you feeling alright?" She asked. I shook my head and shakily pointed at the floor.

"Look," I whispered. "Be careful," I quickly added. She rolled her eyes and got on her knees and lifted up the slab of wood.

"I think you lost It, but okay," She scoffed, she was making no attempt to lower her voice. Her eyes remained on me for a few seconds before her eyes slid down to the hole in the floor.

Her eyes widened, but before the fear could fully register, a slender hand wrapped itself around her throat and violently pulled her down. A loud sickening crack rang out when her head hit the floor but it didn't stop the creature. It kept fulling, her body bending, ripping, and contorting to fit into the small opening in the floor. Blood spurting out randomly as bone ripped through flesh as the creature easily hid her away in the darkness just out of sight. I was shaking violently; my friend was now gone. Blood settled on the floor, but nothing that couldn't be easily cleaned. I stared, scared and helpless. I shakily grabbed my phone and dialed a friend who worked in a hardware store.

"What's up?" My friend June asked.

"Could you help me fix a hole in my floor, quietly?" I asked. I was trying to keep my voice steady and low.

"What happened?" She asked, she sounded worried.

"N-Nothing, I just don't want anyone getting hurt," I stated simply.

"Yeah, of course, I'll bring some things over after work," She offered.

"Thanks, please hurry," I squeaked.

I placed books on the wood to weigh it down as I cleaned the blood up. It only took an hour to clean up all the blood and I went to the bathroom to dump out the bucket of water. I sat on the toilet seat and sighed, I tried gathering my thoughts. After what felt like forever, I heard a knock on the door, making me flinch. I got up and answered it and there stood my friend June. She had her arms full of items and she stumbled in, dropping it on the floor, I quickly hushed and shushed her, I stared at the weighted holes and waited in fear, I let out a sigh of relief.

"What's up?" She asked. She looked worried, but I dare not tell her what I was feeling, knowing what happened to Cindy.

"Oh just, I don't want to bother my neighbor, he's a sweet old man, and I don't want to cause him much more trouble than I already have," I lied, I know I was visibly shaken but I tried to hide it to the best of my abilities. She seemed to accept the answer and began to get to work. I sat and watched her pull the wood up and quietly get to work on measuring the hole.

The door opened and my mum walked in, she gave June an odd look.

"What's going on?" She asked. My heart was in my throat, concerned with the amount of people in the apartment right now, and the amount of noise we were making in front of the open hole.

"Since the guy hasn't come to fix it, I took matters into my own hands," I chuckled. "I just don't want you getting hurt," I continued tensely. She nodded.

"Well, I won't be home long," She said. She went to the kitchen and started making herself some food.

"What the hell is that?" June asked. She squinted down the hole. My mom came to the entryway and we shared a look. I know she saw the fear in my eyes and before she could communicate anything with me, the hand returned, grabbing June's leg and pulling.

My mom's eyes filled with fear as she witnessed what I had seen earlier that day. Within moment's it was clear that June was gone and we watched as the corpse disappeared through the hole. Her knuckles white from clenching her coffee cup so tightly.

"W-We should go," She said quickly and quietly. I pulled the heavy boards June had brought, over the holes.

The Empty House in the Forest

I grinned up at the house as I reached out for the handle. I turned the handle and pushed the door inside. It was heavy and creaked in the frame. The foyer was huge, and there was a tall staircase that led to the second floor. I walked across the foyer; my shoes clicked against the floor. I grabbed the banister and the wood let out a strained cracking noise like it was about to break in half. I took the first steps up the stairs, mind spinning with wonder and enchantment, so many ideas of what me and my mother could achieve here. It was so lovely. I continued to walk up the stairs. The stairs creaked under my weight. The sun shone in, casting the building in a gold tinted glow from the stains on the window. The second floor had about 6 doors, one led to the attic and the rest led to 2 rooms, a bathroom, and 2 closets. 3 doors lining each side of the walkway. I pulled open the doors, peeking in, trying to find the one that led higher into the old creaky house. I got to the third door and pulled it open, stairs leading up to a much dimmer level in the house.

I began climbing up, letting my hands drag along the peeling wallpaper, dust building up on my fingertips. I reached the top and wiped my hands on my jeans. The air smelling soiled and musty.

"Did something die up here?" I asked, scrunching my face at the putrid smell. I tried filling the silence for myself. I walked up to a sheet draped over something big and heavy. I pulled it off revealing multiple boxes. I found the window and pulled the drapes down and the room lit up a bit. Making it feel a lot less scary. I opened the top box and rummaged through the box, only finding old clothes and trinkets. I had to redirect myself to see what else I wanted to check out in the new house. I thought I saw something standing in the corner, it was a grayish white, swollen like it was waterlogged. Loose fabric covered its frame like a robe or a dress. Long brown matted hair hung down, obscuring the face. It was maybe seven feet tall. I paused for just a moment. Before the door creaking caught my attention and I looked at it begin to swing closed. Something made me rush down, catching the door just before it clicked shut.

I looked behind me up the narrow walkway leading upwards. I quietly thanked them because there was nothing there. I tried to call my mother, and she thankfully picked up.

"Hey mom, I'm here, it's kind of scary, when are you going to get here?" I asked, trying to avoid looking at the doorway.

"I should be there in 45," she responded.

"Alright, love you," I said and hung up, I went back down to the first floor and started pulling furniture covers off. It didn't take too long for my mother to show up. We went to the kitchen and I started cooking dinner. I quickly forgot whatever I saw in the attic, happy to have company. Soon dinner was ready and we sat on the floor of the foyer. I happily scarfed down the food. After we finished, we did the dishes and went to our rooms on the second floor. I left my door open, the light in the walkway on, shining a thin line across my floor. I stared at the ceiling; the silence was so different from the white noise of cars in the city. I rolled on my side and looked at my closet, the door was open just a crack as well. For a split second I thought I saw that thing from earlier, standing in the corner of the attic. Just as fast as I thought I saw it, it disappeared. I rolled over, making sure my back was to the closet. I must have just been seeing things.

The next morning, I woke up, my door still cracked. I walked out of the bedroom and went to the bathroom. The door clicked shut and I looked at myself in the mirror and there was that thing I screamed and pulled the door open, getting ready to flee. I tripped on my way out of the bathroom, landing on my hands and knees. I looked behind me and stared into the bathroom, waiting for that thing to walk out, but it never did. My mother came running up the stairs.

"Are you okay?" She called out worriedly. I shakily brought myself to my feet.

"I think so," I said panting. She sighed and left me alone. I went about my routine with the door open, I felt uneasy about having closed. I decided to start unpacking my room, hoping having it feel more homey would make everything less creepy. After a few hours I decided to take a break, I made a lot of progress. I descended the stairs and made my way to the kitchen where my mother was setting up a spice rack.

"How's it going?" I asked with a smile.

"Well," She muttered while reading instructions.

"Have you seen anything funny around the house?" I asked, thinking about this morning in the bathroom. She shook her head. "Really?" I asked. I tried reading her face, she looked perplexed by the paper in front of her. I chuckled and rolled my eyes. "I'm heading back upstairs, later," I said, waving at her before leaving. I returned to my room and laid on my bed. I was exhausted. I stared at the ceiling, my eyes growing heavy. Just as I was slipping away, something shifted in my closet. I was ripped back to reality. I stared at my closet. The door was shut with a hat hanging on the handle. I waited a few minutes, barely blinking, waiting for the slightest sound, the slightest movement. I slowly rose from my bed, careful not to make any noise. I moved to the closet, slowly, being sure to not break the silence. I wrapped my fingers around the doorknob, cringing at the slightest rattle of the knob. I slowly turned it; I braced myself, I jerked the door open and took a sigh of relief. Nothing. I must have just imagined it as I was falling asleep. I sighed and shut the closet door, I felt something fall inside, and I pulled it open.

The door swung open and there stood the lumpy person from the attic and in the mirror this morning. I froze, it grinned down at me. It easily stood at about 7 feet. It wore a light black cloak. I looked down and noticed a large shining blade; white bloated fingers wrapped around the handle. It took a step forward and I slammed the door shut. Loud scraping sounds came from inside the closet. I ran downstairs and grabbed a knife.

"Mom, there's someone with a knife in my closet," I whispered. I saw them last night in the attic. I said softly. I moved to go back upstairs. She grabbed my arm and shook her head. I watched as she dialed 911. She whispered into the phone and I shut the door. Both my mother and I sat behind the island counter. There wasn't a sound besides the creak of old wood supporting this big heavy house. I strained my ears, trying to hear any footsteps or movement. There was nothing. Soon I could hear the whir of police sirens in the distance.

Both my mother and I ran for the front door, running right to the cops getting out of their car. We told them our story and the searched the house. They didn't find anyone. Soon the cops left, not before giving us their personal cards. We went back inside, but I didn't want to go to my room. I didn't want to be alone.

"Do you want to work on unpacking the attic?" Mom asked. I shrugged, not really wanting to do anything anymore out of fear. I followed her to the attic and she made it a point to check every pos-sible place a person could hide before we got to work going through boxes, the silence hung heavy in the air. After a while she stood up and dusting off her pants.

"I'm going to go make us something to eat," She said with a forced smile. I nodded; I didn't want her leaving but there was no way that something was going to appear out of nowhere. I heard her descend the stairs; I sifted through old papers. I sighed and plopped them in a box designated for trash. That's when I noticed the thing slowly walking towards me. It was maybe 3 yards away from me. I jumped backwards, falling over boxes. The thing walked slowly and methodically. Its steps thundered through the attic. I turned over on my hands and knees, trying to make my way to the stairway.

I managed to stumble to my feet and I looked over my shoulder. The thing was a lot closer than I thought it would be, now only a few steps behind me. I felt its footsteps shaking the floor under my feet.

"Holy shit," I whispered. I went to take a few steps forward, but with superhuman speed, it was wrapping its fingers through my hair. I jerked backwards. I screamed as I felt something press against my back. The immediate area felt hot and my muscles twitched and tightened leading me to scream loudly. I felt the pain move deeper into my back. All of a sudden, I was free, I fell forward landing hard on the floor. My hands shield my face with no time to spare. The fast thumps indicated my mom running up the steps. Concern filled her face.

"What's wrong, what happened?" She yelled as she rounded the mini wall at the top of the stairs. She froze and stared at me laying on the floor. "Your bleeding!" She yelled. I looked over my shoulder and saw a quickly growing blood stain on my shirt.

"Oh, my fucking god, it was real!" I shouted.

"What happened?" My mom yelled, balling up an old sheet and pressing it on my back and fumbling for her phone.

"That thing, it was back!" I groaned out through the pain.

"How?" She demanded. "We checked the entire attic!"

"I don't know, it just appeared, you think I could do this to myself?" I hissed. The operator picked up and my mother frantically told them the situation and our address before dropping the phone to the floor.

Dead on Street Corners

I pulled the door open to be greeted by fog, obscuring my view with ashy dulled edges. Buildings merged together in dark gray hills and mountains. I walked out and I couldn't see either end of the street, I sighed and walked in the general direction I should be heading, only making out the faint edges of the sidewalk. I was bundled in a sweatshirt and beanie, fighting off a chilly dull breeze. The air smells rotten, like stale urine, and rotting food. I approached an intersection, mounds hiding the street, a distant ringing of a bell made me quicken my pace, curious what these mounds where I drew near on my way to the trolley stop. Dozens of corpses were piled on top of each other; I was confused and curious, why were there so many dead people laying on these street corners. Only then had I noticed how alone I truly was. I didn't notice any cars on the road, street lamps weren't illuminated.

I looked around and noticed how silent the city truly was. Another, yet closer bell pulled me from my thoughts, making me quickly jog to the trolley stop and wait. My eyes follow the rows of dead on the sidewalk. I heard a faint coughing a few feet away on the sidewalk. Like someone struggling to gasp for air. I looked up the road, the trolley was not yet visible. I ventured further into the fog. I saw a skinny elderly man looking up at me, blood covering his face, it was dried around his eyes, nose and mouth.

"What happened?" I asked. He didn't respond, only grabbed at me weakly with a thin arm. His mouth opened and closed, but once again, no sound came out. "How can I help?" I asked. Nothing, just a blank stare and the hand grabbing for me. I pulled out my phone in an attempt to call for help. The phone rang, it rang for 30 seconds, then a minute. I hung up and tried calling again, all the while the man looked to be growing weaker by the second. The same thing repeated the second time I tried calling.

I heard my trolley coming, and I saw the lights on the front faintly through the fog. I rushed back to the stop, trying to call for help one last time, but once again no one picked up. I boarded and I sat in the window seat. It shifted to go back the way it come, opposite the direction it was supposed to; I leaned out the window into the fog, not seeing anything, not any buildings, no signs and no bridges. As the trolley continued, more bodies on street corners appeared, some of the bodies were bloodied and disemboweled, while others looked merely asleep. I moved to the center of the trolley. I didn't want to see any more people. I watched the trees and street lamps, as the trolley moved past, I was dreading the end of the line. I felt my heart racing in my chest. Unsure what all of this was or meant. Soon the trolley screeched to a stop. I shakily got off the trolley and looked around, the fog was still heavy. I looked around and noticed, there were no bodies.

The Things Hidden on the Island

I sat on the boat with my parents and it skipped across the water, the wind whipping through my hair. I squinted my eyes as the water splashed up and into my face.

"Are you excited, sweetie?" My mother asked. I looked back at her and forced a smile to my face and nodded before looking back to the island. It was rather warm, but quite cloudy. Soon the boat slowed to a halt at a dock. We deboarded the boat and the man who drove us here bid us well for the afternoon. I followed my parents up the wooden dock, the thuds of a dozen people walking towards the island. I drug my eyes over the landscape; taking in the entire view. The island was truly beautiful. The clouds danced violently in the sky, twisting and churning, threatening to ruin the day. I followed my parents across the island to the beach.

When we got there my mum and dad began to set up our area. I waded into the water, scrunching up my face at the chill. I waded in deeper, until the water was around my waist; that's when I felt it. A few drops hitting my face. I looked at the shore and people were looking around and my father was waving his arm at me to call me in from the water. I began to trudge back up to the beach, the water making my bathing suit cling to my body. I shivered as a strong breeze whipped around my body. When I finally got to my parents, they were already heading into the building. I followed and looked behind me and gasped. There was a funnel cloud forming; teasing the surface of the water, threatening to touch down at any moment. My heart jumped into my throat.

"What is this?" A woman asked. It touched the water and skipped onto the land, hovering over a sandy hill. We all watched, all of us frozen in astonishment, as the vortex danced gracefully, dangerously before touching down. It was weak, thin and wispy, but still danger- ous. It bent and curled, struggling to stay alive before disappearing without a trace.

We collectively let out a sigh of relief, I didn't realize I was holding my breath until my chest collapsed under the pressure of my primal need for air. We all looked around at each other, wondering what we should do, if we should go outside or stay in here until the man came back to ferry us off the island. The people began to thin out after about half an hour of waiting. It took my parents about an hour before they were willing to leave. We walked across the island; they were talking about leaving me in some sort of young adult lounge.

"Why can't I hang out with you guys, and do what you guys are doing?" I asked.

"Because we want to do it together," My father answered. I rolled my eyes and sighed. "What?" He asked.

"I just don't get why I have to come along if I'm going to be locked in a cabin with a bunch of people I will never see again," I muttered, already heading towards the young adult lounge.

"I'm sick of you sulking all the time!" My father shouted after me. I ignored him putting my headphones on and entering the cabin where there were a handful of other people. I walked over to a couch and sat down and took in everyone. An older man walked out.

"How are you guys?" He asked as if we were all small kids. There was a murmur around the room of obliged answers. "How about a game?" He asked, holding up a deck of cards.

"I'm good," I said simply.

"Come on," He insisted, a strange, almost evil smile spread across his face, sending a shiver down my spine. The others gathered around the small coffee table in the center of the room. He began to shuffle the cards and explain the rules. I continued to play on my phone until I noticed him dealing me a small pile.

"I said I'm good," I shot firmly. He ignored me and moved onto the next person while I kept tapping away on my phone; I gasped as the phone was ripped from my hand and the man slammed it against the wall.

"You're going to play with us," He growled. My ears were ringing and I felt my pulse in my neck.

"What are you, crazy?" I shouted standing up, getting in his face. He pushed me down so hard that the couch rocked back slightly. I picked up my cards and looked at them, they weren't from a normal deck. They had items on them. What was this game? I stared at my cards puzzled. I sat there and soon the man paused the game to do something in another room. I grabbed his cards and looked at them, trying to figure out what this game was about or how to beat this game so I could leave and find my parents. I put his cards back down and went to the couch, pulling my feet up off the floor and stared at the door he left out of.

He came back and sat back down. He picked up his cards and almost instantly his face twisted in anger.

"Who looked at my cards?" He bellowed. His voice shook the entire lounge. I almost jumped over the back of the couch.

"I did, I want to get this stupid game over with," I said with faux bravery.

"You don't win if you cheat!" He shouted. I was puzzled with how he responded.

"I don't even want to play your stupid game!" I shouted, throwing his cards at him. They rained down to the floor. I stood still, frozen like a stature. The man just stared at me, he grabbed my arm and began to drag me towards a glass door. "Hey don't fucking touch me!" I shouted as he pulled me along. Some of the others started yelling too at this point. He pulled the door open and started outside.

"Where are you taking me?" I shouted trying to pry myself out of his grip. He remained silent and walked out to a small ring of stones. Panic welling in my throat. "Help!" I screamed, hoping someone would come and help me. This man was superhuman. Managing to not be overpowered about 3 young guys trying to remove me from his grip. Soon I felt my legs press against the stone. I looked over my shoulder. It was a well. I couldn't see the bottom. He was pushing me over the edge. The guys switched from trying to free me to trying to keep hold of me so I wouldn't fall over the edge. I felt them grabbing my arms, my legs, and even my hair, trying to keep me from going over the edge. I tried to grab at them, then I felt the hand release on my upper arm. I felt my hands slip from my arms and legs and my vision narrowed to a small circle. It quickly got smaller as the ground rushed towards me, I didn't dare look behind me. I knew what was coming, I rather not know it's coming. I felt tears well in my eyes.

What's in the Freezer

It was a hot summer day, and my friends and I were helping out the man who owned the local party store. He went out of town for a few weeks and hired us to help him clean everything that was spoiled in the small store. It wasn't much but money was money. I sat in front of the cooler, appreciating the chilling sensation in the summer heat. After what felt like hours, I had the urge to explore the back room.

"Let's take a break," I said, standing up and stretching my back. It popped quietly. Andrew and Ollie looked at each other. "What?" I asked. "We hadn't taken a break yet, and we could use something to eat and drink," I said, putting my hands on my hips. They sighed and nodded, standing up and abandoning their bags on the ground. I smiled and turned on my heels walking towards the backroom. There was a door that led to a small one-person bathroom, and a couple huge freezers to store products that aren't due to be upfront yet. I walked up to one of the freezers and pulled it open and saw a bunch of food. I went to the next one and once again it was filled to the brim with food. I don't know why but I was slightly disappointed in there being nothing interesting.

I wandered over to a giant reach in the freezer. I grabbed the handle and pushed the top up and gasped, dropping the lid down. It slammed loudly and I fell back landing hard on my tailbone.

"Guys!" I shouted. They almost instantly appeared in the doorway of the backroom.

"What happened?" Ollie asked. I pointed shakily at the freezer. There was a part of me that wanted to tell him not to open that freezer. My voice refused to go; I opened my mouth but no words came out. My mouth just opened and closed with no words. I wanted to reach out and stop him but my fingers just barely grazed his hand, he was determined to see what I had seen. He walked over and pulled the lid open and his face dropped. All emotion gone. He stared blankly for a few moments before slowly shutting the lid.

"We need to leave," He murmured quietly. In an almost robotic manner, he turned away from the freezer and walked through the doorway leading the way out of the store. Andrew helped me to my feet and he shakily led me to the door. I damn near jumped out of my skin before the old man entered, a big smile plastered to his face, he had a bag in his hand.

"Where are you going?" He asked.

"I-I fell and hurt my ankle, they're taking me home," I said shakily.

"Let me look at it," He said, gesturing at Ollie to bring me over to him. Ollie remained still, staring at him. "What are you doing? Come here," The man said a bit more firmly.

"I-I think it's better if I just go home," I said, scared that I might anger him.

"There isn't any harm in letting me see if I can help," He said. I noticed his large smile was quickly dying away into a sneer. I felt my blood racing in my throat, adrenaline making my thoughts go a mile a minute.

"Really, I'd rather just go home and wrap it myself," I said, my voice breaking off at the end, making my voice seem small and child-like. He grunted and stepped aside, and the three of us almost killed each other trying to fit out the door at the same time. We sprinted to my apartment and ran up the three flights and locked the door behind us.

Abandoned Bookstore

It was a hot afternoon. The large parking lot was gray and cracked with age. It wasn't the best neighborhood, but it wasn't the worst. It was just me and a few friends, you could see people here and there hanging out in front of distant stores, they were far enough away to not want to pay attention to us. We were here for a very special bookstore. The thing that makes this bookstore special is that you don't have to pay for your books, but you do have to leave something of value. According to the tales of this bookshop, there isn't really anyone who runs it; the only time you hear about it is through a friend of a friend. Everyone who has immediately gone has said that they've seen no one, but doesn't want to risk just stealing. Given the area it is shocking that there aren't more thefts, but according to tales about this place, everyone who steals or leaves a less than worthy offering, they get haunted.

My friends approached the door, I hung back; I was a very superstitious person, hearing all the stories had the skin on the back of my neck on end. They pulled the door open and there was a swell of excitement in my chest. Stepping through the door was anticlimactic. The door rattled shut behind me, and an old bell rattled above the door. We stood there, waiting, trying to see if there really weren't any workers there. The silence was eerie. When you're so used to the ambient noise of the cars on the road, people chattering on the sidewalk, and the hum of signs, the silence is almost painful. There was dust covering everything and the bookshelves weren't even labeled. There were books scattered on top of shelves, on the floor and on the tables. The windows were yellow and dirty, you couldn't see outside and likewise, you couldn't see inside.

We dispersed to look at various shelves, stacks, and clusters of books. Our pockets and bags lined with old jewelry, video games, and other valuables. There wasn't anything that caught my eye at first, it just looked like a typical used bookstore. I found myself wandering away from my group of friends, lingering closer and closer to the back of the store. Curious about other books, and possibly finding a clerk or any kind of worker. There was a desk where an employee would sit and a door behind it. The store was dimly lit at best, so I couldn't see past the deep brown, yet dusty doorway. I listened to my better instincts and returned to the group with a chill down my spine. I didn't say anything to them but continued looking at books.

I looked back over at the door and let out a yelp when I saw a shadowy figure at the desk. Everyone's eyes fell to me before following my gaze to the doorway, but when I looked back there wasn't anyone there.

"I-I thought there was someone standing there," I murmured. Everyone looked at me and followed my gaze. When I looked back there was no one there. "I swear I saw something," I murmured, staring at the door, straining my eyes.

"Here you go," He muttered, he walked over to the desk, I stood frozen, partially from shock and partially from fear. He jumped on the counter, leaving footprints in the gunk on top of it. All our friends' eyes were on him. My eyes couldn't help but dart around, searching for the figure I saw in the doorway.

"Maybe we should leave?" I asked. I felt uneasy, scared, sick to my stomach.

"Why don't we look for this mysterious figure?" Jared asked, still standing on the counter.

"That sounds like fun," Jayla said. She revealed that she was making me uncomfortable. Jared promptly leapt down to the floor on the other side with a loud yet hollow thud. A breeze on my neck caused me to whip around, but there was nothing. I felt like throwing up, it wasn't from the stuffy room, or the dust, or even what I ate, something was off, very off, but I couldn't bring myself to leave my friends here. Jared grinned as he turned the flash light on his phone on, holding it under his face much like you would a flashlight when telling ghost stories around a campfire. He turned around and held the light out in front of him, it seemed to be yet another room full of books. He turned around multiple times, looking up and down, all around, yet he still found nothing. I felt my tension ease, there wasn't anything there after all.

Jayla was next to make her way into the room. I remained in the front portion, I looked back at the door, it was just a few feet away, but it also felt like miles, several inches could make the difference of living through a paranormal experience. I found myself inching backwards as they looked at all the books that weren't displayed. One step back, again, and again, slowly but surely making my way to the door. I felt the knob jab my lower back, causing me to reflexively look behind me. When I turned back around the store was empty. The shelves and tables were bare, not a single book in sight. I spun around to try and open the door, but it wasn't working. I looked over my shoulder and the room was still empty, then it occurred to me; where were my friends? I spun my head to look in the room they were in, it was still full of books, and they were still looking at them, only the shadow figure was behind them. I tried opening the door again.

"Do you think this mp3 player is enough for this book?" Jayla asked Jared. He turned to look at her and that's when he noticed the figure.

"Guys!" I shouted as I fumbled with the door. They didn't hear me though; their eyes were on the figure. It was tall and shadowy. It loomed over them, silently staring down at the teenagers. It took Jared only moments to sprint out of the room.

"Open the door!" He shouted at me.

"I can't!" I yelled back, turning the handle and pushing and pulling it violently. I was shoved out of the way, and I fell to the ground scraping my elbow on the dusty floor. I looked back at Jayla to see that she had fallen to her knees, staring at the figure. Jared gave up and whipped around to also look at Jayla. I grabbed a book and tried throwing it at the window, but it bounced off like the window was made of rubber or Plexiglas.

I saw the thing slowly approaching Jayla as she stared at it in horror. She finally moved, falling backward and scooting backwards, disappearing out of sight. The thing approached her, maintaining a slow speed. I jumped to my feet and once again started pulling on the door. I noticed the lock and unlocked it and fell out of the door. The light was blinding as I fell onto my hands and knees. I rolled onto my back to look at the door; it was closed. It looked as if we never had entered, I stood up and grabbed the doorknob and opened the door, and it was empty, completely cleared out. No books or shelves. Just a dusty floor and four walls. I shakily shut the door and turned around to go home.

Lost At a Friends

I was asked to look after my friend's pets while she was out of town. I stood in the foyer checking text messages from my friend, she needed to tell me how to find the way to her apartment. Her response was a set of directions letting me know how easy it was to find her apartment. The directions were straight forward, go through the nearest door, take the stairs and her apartment would be 6B. I looked around, there were about 3 doors, one ahead of me down a hall, one down a hall to my left and a short haul to my right. I decided to take that door because it's the closest door to me. I made my way down the hall; my shoes tapping on the linoleum floor. I grabbed the door handle, and it was cold against my hand. The door creaked as I opened it. I found myself overlooking a stairwell. I followed the stairs up several flights. My thighs already burned, I wondered how she could stand to do this almost every day.

When I finally reached the door, I was out of breath. I pushed the door open expecting to see a hallway of units, but my heart sank when I entered yet another stairwell. The stairs hugged the wall, but something froze me in my tracks. Near the bottom there was what looked like a glass wall, It looked like an aquarium. The water was a beautiful cerulean; the bottom was filled with green water shrubs.

There were bubbles floating to a surface that was beyond my sight. There were small fishes swimming around. The thing that caught my eye was this large jellyfish. It looked like it was about the size of a car. The color was a peachy mustard tone. It just hovered in the tank, not moving. I watched it closely, trying to determine whether it was real or not. Its tentacles moved and swayed with the water, it looked almost ethereal. Almost as quickly as I blinked, its entire body slammed into the glass.

I stood frozen, unsure what to do, lost in this strange building, a stranger. It slammed into the glass once more. My heart began to race. I looked at the floor from the overlook; it was about 4 floors down. The jellyfish slammed into the glass one last time before a white spider web shot from the impact point. Within moments the glass collapsed in on itself and the water rushed out onto the floor. The jellyfish lay on the ground, still and lifeless. I stared at it, a massive, slimy blob. I made my way to the edge of the stairs, getting ready to make my way down. Almost as if it knew my intentions the thing sprung to life, shooting up to slam against the ceiling. I let out a shrill yelp of terror at the booming thud of the massive creature hitting the old wood and concrete. I stepped away, slowly backing towards the doorway.

At this point I heard my heart in my ears, scared of what this thing could do, what it might be able to do to me. Yet another shriek left my throat when I felt the cold door handle against the base of my back. I whipped around quickly ripping the door open and ran outside. The sound of the thing slamming against the ceiling muted the second the door closed. It was like since the door was closed it was a completely different universe. There was another door across the hall from me, I ran to it, hoping to find something identifiable. I grabbed the door handle and when I opened it, it was just a regular apartment building hallway. I stepped inside, letting the door swing shut behind me. I walked down the hall, looking at the apartment numbers hoping to find my friend's apartment. Eventually after what felt like hours of walking in circles, I found it. I opened the door with the key and the apartment was a mess. There were clothes everywhere.

I stepped into the apartment looking around, there was absolutely no sense of organization. I approached a nearby shelf. It had a basket with a black shirt thrown over it. I found a handful of marbles in the basket. There were a few other odds and ends like ChapStick and coins. I picked up the marbles and rolled them around in my hand. I heard a door in the apartment open and close making me jump. I looked deeper into the apartment. I saw my friend enter the kitchen from a door shrouded in shadow. She looked spaced out.

"Claire?" I called out to her. I put my hands in my pocket, forgetting the marbles were in my hand and they clattered in my pocket. She didn't respond, she just looked at me. She looked confused as if she thought she knew me from somewhere but couldn't remember where. "Claire, it's me," I said.

"What are you doing here?" She asked. Her voice was soft, it sounded as if it was in the wind, not coming from her.

"You asked me to house sit for you," I responded, stepping closer.

"Oh..." She murmured. I stared at her, the hair on the back of my neck stood on edge.

"I'm going to go," I murmured, backing away slowly. My chest was tight, I didn't realize I was holding my breath. I tripped over my own feet and fell. When I looked back up, I was outside again. It was dark, and the concrete was wet. The sun was just barely dipping under the horizon. The world was a dark, ashy Cerulean.

Traveled

I found myself walking up a drab sidewalk. I was meeting a longtime friend at a hotel bar to catch up. I was itching to take the edge off in some way. I quit smoking and I felt like a fiend, if I wasn't going to smoke I might as well drink. I couldn't help but feel mildly disoriented, this was a new area in the city that I rarely if ever went to, mainly because it was out of the way. The sky was a threatening dark gray, any second it could start pouring rain, and all I had was a sweatshirt to protect me. The buildings were in a questionable condition, they weren't in the worst shape, but not the best shape. There were people drinking cheap beers on the sidewalk and one of them clearly had peed their pants at some point in the day. I tried to keep my head down. The wind whipped around me as it continued to threaten the rain. Soon I saw the hotel and I began to walk faster. I was eager to get inside. When I entered you could tell it was a fancy hotel.

I looked around and saw a hallway with a sign with Maury's Cocktail Lounge written on it. I walked down the hallway and found myself at a modest bar. There were only a handful of tables with white clothes on top of them. The lights were dim, and the liquor shelf was backlit. I sat down at the bar and waited for my friend. I hadn't seen him in months since we stopped working at the same job. I ordered a beer and kept an eye on the entryway. After about 20 minutes I saw him enter, I happily jumped up and went over to hug him. We sat at the bar and it took about an hour to catch up. Something seemed off though. He looked like Keaten, but he didn't act like Keaten. I figured it was because he works a better job now, so maybe that was it, though it was almost like I was talking to a poorly replicated version of him. There were little things he would get wrong about the stories we would reminisce about.

After about an hour or two it was time for us to say our farewells. I put cash down for the beers I had and stood. He also quickly stood.

"Are you leaving?" He asked. "So soon?" He asked. I nodded.

"Yeah, I got to get home, you know how it is with early start times," I responded, chuckling slightly. I smoothed my clothes down and turned to head out.

"Don't you want to share a joint like the good ole' days?" He asked me, pulling out a tube with a pre-rolled joint in it.

"I would, but I'm trying to quit smoking," I chuckled, rubbing the back of my neck. He looked a bit frustrated, and this made me feel uneasy. I slowly turned and began to head back down the hallway. It seemed different than before. I heard footsteps behind me, I tried my best to look over my shoulder and I saw that Keaten was following me. I tried to calm myself down, telling myself that he is also just leaving just like me. Since we finished hanging out, he had no other reason to be in the bar anymore.

I couldn't help but feel uneasy about him. Something just seemed off, it was like a sixth sense, a third eye. The lobby wasn't busy, just a few workers sitting and chatting with each other, just idle chats that we all have at our own jobs. I sat down at one of the chairs and started messing with my phone, checking the bus schedule, but mostly just taking note of what Keaten is going to do. I watched him out of the corner of my eye, and I could see that he was staring me down, trying to stay out of direct line of sight. I stood up and walked over to the group of employees.

"Hi, I just left the bar, I was wondering if there was a bathroom I could use before I go home," I asked politely.

"Of course, it should be down that hall, and you can't miss them, they are unisex bathrooms," one of the girls responded pointing at the hallway.

"Thank you," I said before going down the hallway. Once again, I heard the light taps of footsteps behind me. I felt my heart racing in my chest. As I walked, I saw a cart full of linens, without thinking I pulled myself into the cart and buried myself in the cloth and held my breath.

I heard his footsteps getting closer. It was almost like there was an echo with each step he took. His steps kept getting louder, like he was intentionally trying to menace me. Soon they were next to the linens I actively hid in. Thankfully he didn't stop, he kept walking. Soon his footsteps grew quiet, I tried my best to quietly lift myself out of the basket. At this moment the rumpled fabric sounded like a thunderstorm. I found myself sprinting down the hallway. When I reached the end of it I quietly and quickly thanked the employees, they seemed confused but nodded me along. I quickly walked out the door and went on my way. I kept looking over my shoulder and trying to see if I could see him. I ducked into a convenience store to try and kill some time. I found myself by the book section, looking out the window to see if he had passed it. After about 20 minutes of roaming about the store, I finally left and went on my merry way home.

I don't know what told me to do this, but I felt the need to turn around, there I saw him sitting in his car. His eyes were locked on me, boring a hole through my soul. I turned to continue going home. I decided to take more turns than I usually would. Sometimes going in circles, turning around, and stopping for long periods of time. He followed me during all of it. I felt alone, I couldn't get help, there was no one around to help me. I decided to approach the car. I reached into my pocket and grabbed my pepper spray and held it tight. When I got to his window, he rolled it down, a cloud of familiar smelling smoke rolled out.

"What's up?" He smiled up at me. You could tell that he was high just by the look on his face.

"Why are you following me?" I asked, I tried to keep my composure, I didn't want to make him feel threatened.

"I just want to make sure you got home safe," he gave me a menacing smile.

"I can get home on my own just fine, I know how to handle myself," I sneered. I kept eyeing the joint in his hand.

"You want some?" He offered, sticking the joint out to me. I looked around.

"Would you leave me alone if I did?" I asked, narrowing my eyes at him.

"Of course," he said with a more genuine, kind smile. I hesitantly reached out and took it from his fingers. I shakily held the joint between my lips and took a deep breath in. I immediately felt relaxed. I quickly handed it back.

"I'm going to go home now, and you'll leave me alone, right?" I asked. He nodded and drove off. I continued my way home. I felt so relaxed and calm.

Hallways or Mirrors

I found myself in a hallway, I didn't know how I got here, just that I was here. I looked around and the walls were a dark Mahogany and there was a crimson carpet on the floor. I decided to follow the hall down, I could tell that there were several archways indicating that there were doorways of sorts there. I began walking down the hallway, observing the floors and walls, trying to figure out what this place is. I came to the first arch way. When I looked through it, there was a smaller hallway leading to a landing with a banister and another archway perfectly across from me. I noticed something as I walked past, someone walked past as well. I backed up and saw them back up as well. When I started to walk down the second hallway, they did too, that's when I realized, it was me. How could that be? I approached the banister and the second me did as well. They looked just as confused as I felt. I waved and they waved just as I did, like a perfect mirror, but only they looked so real, like I was looking at a doppelganger.

I found myself leaning over the banister and they did just the same. I squinted to try and make out more details and they did too. I fell backwards, they were like me in every way, down to every freckle, and the one slightly larger nostril than the other. Once again, they mirrored every move I made. I backed down the short hallway and jumped when my back hit the wall. I turned and continued down the hallway, when I approached the archway, it led down another long hallway. It seemed to go on forever. I took a breath and decided the risk was worth trying to get out of this place. I started down the hallway. As I walked, I noticed there was movement just beyond the shadows. I sped up trying to get close enough to it. It seemed forever just out of sight. When I turned around the hallway went on forever just as it did in front of me, where I came from vanished as if it never existed. I walked back, hoping that maybe it was just a trick of the eyes. I walked much longer than I did to get as far as I did. I turned back around and started sprinting up the hallway.

I desperately wanted to find something. After only about 5 minutes of running down the hallway I saw another archway come into view. Once I reached it I walked through it. Once more, I saw myself mirrored.

"Hello?" I shouted. No voice came out of the mirrored version of me. I waved at it and it waved at me. I looked around the large room, looking for a way to get to the other side. I noticed a ladder that led to an overhead walkway. I looked to see if there was one on the other side. There wasn't. What was going to happen if the mirrored version of me can't climb. Will it glitch, will it go crazy. I approached the ladder and climbed up. When I reached the walkway and turned around. I couldn't help but scream. I saw a mirror of the walkway I was on. I fell backwards and my mirrored version also fell backwards. I looked down and there was no longer a mirror version of me. I began to feel dizzy; the darkness went on forever, nothing to break it up, no light and no wind. There was no longer anything below me. Nothing above me. I was just stuck up here, with whatever the thing across from me is.

Boarding School

My father left me in the office after filling out the paperwork. I was now stuck here until I was picked up by a parent or guardian. I looked at the unfamiliar office staff. Their faces looked emotionless, almost plastic. Their movements were robotic. They didn't even notice I was still there. I looked out the large window in the office and I was able to see the lunch room, some lockers, and a few classroom doors. I didn't even receive a map upon getting signed in. I gave one last glance to the office staff before stepping out into the hallway. There were kids walking around, standing and chatting, getting things out of their lockers. I walked about, looking for a teacher, anyone who could help me. All I have is a list of classes. Soon I spotted an adult standing outside of a classroom.

"Hello, excuse me, I'm new and can't find my class," I explained. I had my schedule in hand. They didn't say anything, just stood there staring. I was a bit puzzled at first, waiting for an answer. They just stared ahead blankly. I looked around looking for someone else who might be able to help me and the halls were empty. There were no kids in the hallways, there was no sound. On top of all this the halls were pure white, the floors, walls and lockers. I looked inside the classroom the teacher was in front of and there were students sitting silently, looking at the white board. They said nothing, and they didn't move. They were almost like hyper realistic mannequins. Their chests didn't rise or fall like when people breathe. They didn't blink, they just stared. I looked at the room number of my first class and the number pasted onto the doorway.

I sighed and started on the mission to find my classroom, knowing no one would help me. It felt like I was walking around forever trying to find the room. Up and down pristine white hallways. There were no signs of dirt or dust. I wondered what kind of school this was. I doubted that a bunch of teenagers would willingly be this well behaved, even out of the best bunch of teens you'll have the reckless ones. It took me about an hour to finally locate my classroom. When I stepped inside there was a teacher sitting at the desk, all the students in the classroom were seated elegantly at their desks. Their ankles crossed just so, their hands folded on top of their desks, and large plastic smiles on their faces. Their eyes held no emotion. I approached the desk, and the teacher didn't look at me, just stared at the students.

"Hello," I said, my voice echoed off the walls, it was the only sound in the school. The teacher didn't respond. I followed the teacher's gaze to the back of the classroom.

"Sit down!" A voice boomed. I jumped and almost fell on the floor, when I looked over my shoulder back at the teacher, he was now looking at me. My heart was racing in my chest. When I looked back up to the students, they were all staring at me; unsettling smiles were no longer there, they were replaced by scowls. I saw an empty chair in the back right corner of the classroom. I made my way to the seat. I was hyper aware of my footsteps, how they tapped against the floor, I sat down at my desk and looked at all the students once more. They were still all looking at me, some were now twisted in their chairs, the same scowls still on their faces. I looked at the whiteboard but there was nothing written. I just sat and waited, waiting for the teacher or the students to move, but it was as still as stone.

I ended up pulling out a notebook and doodling, watching the clock tick away. I noticed each time I looked up some of the students would no longer be looking at me and facing the whiteboard. I kept looking around, hoping to catch them moving in the slightest. They remained perfectly still. When the bell rang, I decided not to go to my next class. This was all too weird, and I had to get out of here. I walked out of the classroom and rushed back up the hallway. I was thankful that I was slightly more familiar with the layout. I found myself getting turned around in some areas, I saw one of the side exits to the school. I walked out, instinctually looking over my shoulder. There was no one watching, and I stumbled out into the chilly spring air. I looked around and it was dark out, I looked at my phone and saw that it was only 5 in the morning. I lost so much time. I turned to face the school, stumbling backwards on my own feet.

I turned around and began walking. I didn't know where I was going but I couldn't stay at the school. There was something deeply wrong with that school. There were large dorms, all the lights were off, leaving the sidewalks lit by street lights which were spaced so widely apart there were completely dark patches of grass and concrete. I felt like holding my breath, I was trying to make as little noise as possible. The grass was wet with morning dew, the fog was thick and heavy, it was refreshing in my lungs. I soon got to a bridge, it was a bridge to freedom for this strange place.

Trick or Treat

I found myself walking down a street that was both familiar and unfamiliar. There were buildings I recognized but also buildings I didn't. The way the sidewalk was designed I knew exactly where I was, but everything also seemed slightly off. There was a large area about the size of a small park. There were pumpkins hanging from the streetlights. There were leaves all over the ground and piled up against the plant basins. There were haystacks and gourds all about to give everything that much more of an autumnal aesthetic. I walked past, I had to go grocery shopping and I know the store will be empty because it's Halloween night. I would be able to get in, get my groceries and get out hopefully in under half an hour. After about twenty minutes of walking past decorated streets filled with children running about with bags and parents begrudgingly following them. Insisting to wait to eat candy until they got home.

There were teenagers meandering about, in costumes, but they didn't really seem interested in getting candy, they seemed more interested in taking photos in their costumes and getting good photo ops. When I got to the store it looked busier than I thought it was going to be. I wasn't too upset by it though because it still seemed fairly desolate. I stepped inside and grabbed a basket and began making my way through the center of the store where all the isles feed into. Something seemed a bit off, I made sure I had my phone, wallet, and keys; those weren't missing. I looked up at the signs for the isles and they were all blank. They hung over the isles, numberless, no descriptions of where to get what you need. There were other people who were going about their shopping as usual. I shrugged it off, it won't be too hard to infer what is down what aisle based on what I can see. I slowed my pace walking up the center, glancing down each aisle.

I knew the store well, but sometimes when you eat something with ingredients, you're unfamiliar with it and you do get stumped. The only thing that had thrown me off though, is that the isles were mixed up. You would have soup and ramen with the noodles. The sauces with the dairy, eggs with bread, soda with the clothing. Nothing was where it ought to be, and some of these combinations could get people sick if they bought the items without knowing any better. I bought most of my items but made a mental note to go to a different store the next day. I was unsettled and I just wanted to return home and make myself dinner. When I walked out of the store, the parking lot was completely empty. Yet another off-putting thing to make my day stranger. I tried my best to shrug off the whole store experience and went on my merry way home, as I walked, I kept my eyes to the sky.

It was pitch black outside; the only light was the faint orange glow of the street lights. Small circles of light illuminated the light gray concrete. Bits of trash and glass strewn about. I noticed that there were no longer people out and about. There were no cars on the road, no kids, teenagers, or adults. There wasn't even your occasional homeless person. I was tempted to get a ride the rest of the way because I was officially scared of what was going on. I pulled out my phone and it was dead. It shouldn't be dead; I left the house with sixty percent and I was barely on my phone. The last time I was on my phone I had about fifty percent left. I shrugged it off and kept walking. When I approached the concrete square, all of the gourds were rotten. The hay was strewn about. I felt like there was something just beyond the darkness, staring at me, watching my every move.

I slowly walked through, my eyes drifting side to side. I felt whatever creature in the shadows boring a hole through my soul. I felt paralyzed, just staring into the threatening darkness. It was staring into an abyss and just knowing in your heart something is staring back. I took a deep breath and took one step forward. My heart sat in my throat; I was ready to throw out whatever the contents of my stomach were. I heard a sound come from behind me and I turned around. I saw a road covered in brinks. They were old and dirty, the color of ancient blood; dark and grungy. At the end of the brick road stood a school made of pale-yellow bricks. All the lights were off, and the shrubs look like they hadn't been tended to in years. Right next to the concrete sidewalk that encompassed the school, were small torches that were lit. They swung and swayed in the wind.

I looked up in the sky and it was no longer pitch black, it was a dark Cerulean. I felt the breeze over my face, the air smelled smokey like there was a bonfire in the neighborhood. I took a deep breath, allowing my heart to settle. I heard the dead leaves skitter in the wind, in the hop, skip, and slide of the leaves, it sounds like the hop, skip and step of a person. I whipped around to see a dimly lit street of houses. Kids, teens, and parents roamed about trying to fill their bags with candy.

Gums

I was on my way to work; it was dark out and foggy. The street was empty, it was too early for people to be out and about. There are perks to having a job that starts ungodly early. The air felt fresh in my lungs, it was still cool out, there were no ambient sounds of people talking and car engines. I enjoyed these moments, I felt like I had the entire city to myself. Unfortunately, despite being in such a soothing and calm environment, my chest still felt tight with stress.

All I want is to be able to sit here forever and never worry about stress. My jaw clenched because of the massive amount of anxiety I had. I tried my best to keep my mouth relaxed but I couldn't unclench my teeth. I unclenched my teeth and ran my tongue over my teeth, trying to feel the texture. I felt my tongue catch on something sharp in my mouth.

I didn't know what it was. I hadn't eaten any hard foods this morning and I brushed my teeth both last night and this morning. I had no idea what it would be. My tongue was stuck, much like a piece of meat on a barbed blade. I tried pulling my tongue and pain shot through my jaw. I was confused, scared, and alone. I tried pulling my tongue again and it came loose, along with some hard smooth object. I spit them into my hand. Low and behold, it was bloody teeth. I reached into my mouth to feel around with my fingers how many teeth I had lost. As I drug my fingers around my mouth, I felt the soft, squishy, bloody pallet my teeth rested in. Sharp nubs are the only thing that would indicate that at some point teeth resided there. I tried pushing my teeth back into their sockets. I was alone in the middle of a sidewalk. No one was there to help or even comfort me.

The teeth just kept falling out of my mouth all over again, I couldn't get them to stick in. My vision blurred as I was getting ready to cry. My face was hot, a breakdown was stewing underneath my skin, I was trying so hard to maintain composure. I wanted so badly to not freak out. My hands were shaking so badly. What would people think of me just missing my teeth? What would I do at work? At least I could hide it with a mask, but they would know something is up the second I would try speaking and I had a violent list due to having no teeth. I could buy one of those veneers online and make it look like I have better teeth than the ones that fell out of my face. So many thoughts were racing through my mind. I dropped to my knees to try and collect myself.

I took a deep breath in and a deep breath out. I felt my heart drumming in my chest, I heard the blood rushing in my ears. Hot tears rolled down my face thinking about all the what ifs while I tried desperately to put the teeth back in my mouth. Just as I was thinking things couldn't get any worse, before I had even developed a solution for the problem in its current state, it escalated. More porcelain white teeth came tumbling out of my mouth, one by one, they tumbled into my hands and lap. They made feeble clicks as they hit the gray concrete. What was once a pristine light gray was now stained in droplets of blood. I tried gathering up every tooth, but I had no idea how many I had lost, I had no idea how I looked. All I knew is that I was missing a lot of teeth, I was bleeding profusely, and I had no idea how to solve this problem.

www.ingramcontent.com/pod-product-compliance
Lightning Source LLC
Chambersburg PA
CBHW072240150726
48002CB00005B/2182